When Geoffrey McSk[...]
found an old motion-pic[...]
containing a dusty film in[...]
He screened the film and was transfixed by
the flickering image of a man in a jaunty pith helmet,
baggy Sahara shorts and special desert sun-spectacles.
The man had an imposing macaw and a clever-looking
camel, and Geoffrey McSkimming was mesmerized
by their activities in black-and-white Egypt, Peru,
Greece, and other exotic locations.

Years later he discovered the identities of the trio,
and he has spent much of his time since then retracing
their footsteps, interviewing surviving members of the
Old Relics Society, and gradually reconstructing these
lost true tales which have become the enormously
successful Cairo Jim Chronicles.

Geoffrey McSkimming was inspired to write
Cairo Jim in Search of Martenarten after getting
sunstroke in the Valley of the Kings.

For Belinda,
who knows why

CAIRO JIM

IN SEARCH OF MARTENARTEN

A Tale of Archaeology, Adventure and Astonishment

GEOFFREY McSKIMMING

WALKER
BOOKS

First published in Great Britain 2006 by Walker Books Ltd
87 Vauxhall Walk, London SE11 5HJ

2 4 6 8 10 9 7 5 3 1

Text © 1991 Geoffrey McSkimming
Cover illustration © 2006 Martin Chatterton

This book has been typeset in Plantin

Printed in Great Britain by
Cox & Wyman Ltd, Reading, Berkshire

British Library Cataloguing in Publication Data:
a catalogue record for this book is available from the British Library.

ISBN-13: 978-1-4063-0020-8
ISBN-10: 1-4063-0020-9

www.walkerbooks.co.uk

▲▲▲▲▲ CONTENTS ▲▲▲▲▲

1

IN THE VALLEY OF THE KINGS

FAR AWAY IN UPPER EGYPT, in a place known as the Valley of the Kings, another hot night had settled like a heavy feather quilt over the rugged landscape, and all through the Valley the ancient dust was thick with silence.

The air barely stirred in little breezes wafting timidly across from the river Nile.

Everything was stony and unmoving.

Everywhere was quiet as the grave.

Then Doris, the brave and colourful hieroglyph-reading macaw who was Cairo Jim's constant companion in his archaeological pursuits, sucked long and hard on a snail. "*Sluuuurrrrp.*"

Cairo Jim, that well-known archaeologist and poet, discoverer of the famous Jocelyn Hieroglyphs, celebrated adventurer and collector of antiquated things, turned from the small table where he was about to start writing into his journal. "Doris," he said quietly, yet with an air of gentle authority, "if I've told you once, I've told you a hundred times, chew them, do not suck them. The noise is dreadful."

"I shall endeavour," Doris squawked, shifting on her perch.

"What would Miss Osgood think if she were here?"

"But she's not. She won't be back for three weeks."

"It's a shame Valkyrian Airways has altered her route. Still, I expect she'll find things to keep her occupied in Morocco."

Doris thought for a moment. "Does that mean she won't be visiting us as much?"

Jim turned up the flame in his kerosene lamp and returned to his journal. "Yes, I suppose it does," he said softly.

"Good," thought Doris as she chewed her escargot. "It's not that I dislike Jocelyn Osgood – she's good fun sometimes, especially when we play gin rummy (she's so easy to beat!) but what drives me off the twig is when she insists on tying ribbons in my plumage. Yerk. If I were meant to have ribbons I'd've been born a poodle. And when she's here, Jim always shaves every day. For goodness' sake, an archaeologist has more important things to do than shave. Why, if he spent all his time shaving we'd never find the Tomb of Martenarten. And he'd never get any poems written."

Then, as she pecked up another snail from her antique snail bowl, she thought about what she'd look like if in fact she *were* a poodle. She imagined herself with a wet nose and curly white hair and a silly tail and she saw a big perfumed woman taking her for walks on a pink leash, and the image was so overwhelmingly ghastly she let out a horrendous screech which echoed through the Valley. "*Reeeeaaaarrrrk!*"

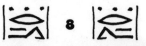

"Shhh!" whispered Cairo Jim. "You'll wake the dead."

"My apologies," prowked Doris.

The archaeologist-poet dipped his pen into the inkwell and, taking a deep breath, set it to a clean blank page in his journal:

Friday, August 17.

Seven-thirty p.m.

Another hot day of fruitless activity, just like yesterday and the day before that. And the one before that. And like last week and the week before and last month and the month before it.

It is exactly three months since we came to the Valley. We have dug and tunnelled for the lost Tomb, but all we have uncovered so far are worthless bracelets and stone scarabs – which seem to be popping up all over this great land – and a black-and-white photograph of Buzz Aldrin (it's quite a good shot of him dancing on the moon and I have pinned it up inside my tent).

Today I had word from Cairo – that most exciting of cities. Apparently two weeks ago Captain Neptune Bone gave a lecture to the Old Relics Society in which he stated there was no way we would discover Martenarten down here in the Valley, and claimed that the Tomb is located somewhere closer to Cairo. I don't know where he gets his information – probably from that unreliable raven of his, Desdemona – but apparently those present at the lecture warmly clapped him at the end of it. It's a sad thing when your colleagues take notice of so untrustworthy a man as Bone.

But I shall persevere. We will not give up or put down our shovels until Martenarten is found.

I only have one small fear: that our generous and wealthy patron, Gerald Perry (Esquire), will run out of funds if we do not make the discovery soon. Up until now he has been incredibly kind and supportive, but his wallet is surely not a bottomless pit – unlike our excavation – and I worry that he might not be able to afford the project for much longer.

It is getting late now and so I shall go to bed. We have to be up early in the morning as usual and I don't think Doris is having enough sleep. Her feathers are looking a little wan.

I hope with all my heart that tomorrow we will stumble on something astonishing.

By the time Jim laid down his pen, Doris had finished her snails and was teetering on her perch in her usual after-dinner state of fed-up bliss.

"Finished?" she flarped at him.

"Finished," said Jim. "And now to sleep."

"To sleep, perchance to dream…"

"Very good, Doris."

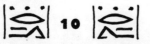 10

"Shakespeare," said the feathered one.

"Goodnight."

"Raaaark."

Cairo Jim picked up his journal and took the kerosene lamp into his tent, where he found Brenda the Wonder Camel sitting on the floor playing solitaire. He put the camel out, picked up the scattered playing cards, got into his night galabiyya and cleaned his teeth thoroughly. Then, after straightening the photograph of Buzz Aldrin, he climbed into his rickety old camp bed where he quickly fell into a deep and fuzzy slumber.

And the Valley of the Kings whispered its secrets of antiquity into the still night air, and somewhere in the sleepy darkness the Tomb of Martenarten was waiting to be discovered.

2

A CLUE IN GURNA VILLAGE

TWO DAYS LATER it was Sunday and the sun beat down mercilessly over the Valley.

For Doris, Sunday was always the best day. She looked forward to her weekly swim in the Nile and she looked forward even more to the scrumptious honey-and-fig shergold cakes Jim bought at the little tea-shop owned by Mrs Amun-Ra, a stout woman who was always glad to see them. Lately Mrs Amun-Ra had been making special shergold cakes just for Doris, filled with snails imported from Malawi, and the yellow-and-blue macaw thought they were the best things since sliced bread – which is a silly saying because Doris hated sliced bread, but after eating these beak-watering delicacies she couldn't care less what tired old sayings sprang to her ecstatic mind.

This morning, as she waited for Jim to get ready for their regular excursion, she sat in the dust with Brenda the Wonder Camel, trying to teach the silent beast how to play canasta. Brenda tried and tried to understand, but mathematics had never been her strong point and the numbers on the cards muddled her terribly. She preferred her usual game of solitaire, when she knew that if she made a mistake nobody would be around to laugh at her. She may

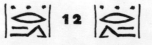

not have been the greatest card player in the world, but she was full of Wonder in many other ways, and Jim would not be without her for all the gold in Egypt.

At last he was ready. He emerged from his tent putting on his special desert sun-spectacles and pith helmet. "Morning, Doris. Morning, Brenda."

Doris rerked and flew up onto his shoulder, while Brenda gave a salutatory snort.

"Ah, you're saddled already," Jim said to the Wonder Camel.

"Thanks to me," said Doris. "If we'd waited for you, we'd still be here at lunchtime. I nearly broke my beak trying to lift the confounded thing over her humps." Doris was always a little testy when she was hungry, even more so if there were shergold cakes to look forward to.

"Thank you, Doris. Your efforts never go unnoticed." And he gave her plumage an affectionate tousle.

"Well, let's go then," she squawked, blushing underneath her feathers.

Jim mounted Brenda and, with Doris perched in a commanding position, off they rode.

The Mortuary Temple of Queen Hatshepsut was already swarming with tourists and souvenir vendors, even though it was not yet nine o'clock. Jim, Doris and Brenda looked down on it as they descended the narrow path from the Valley to the village of Gurna. "A good day for the soft-drink sellers," said Jim, to which Doris gave a shattering screech that ricocheted down into the

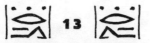

Temple grounds, causing not a few German tourists to run for cover.

As Brenda lumbered past the crumbling statues of the Colossi of Memnon, Cairo Jim became wistful. "Ah, Doris," he sighed. "I would give anything I own to travel back to the good old days. Back to the days when every morning at dawn those Colossi used to sing in the early mists. When the Romans came here, they heard the blasts of trumpets blaring from the statues' heads. The Greeks said it was the chanting of an almighty voice. They were sure it was Memnon greeting his mother Aurora. Alas, now the mighty figures are silent. The noise is no more. But would it not be great if in our lifetimes, Memnon were to return and – and—"

"Would you really give *anything* you own?" Doris asked.

"Anything."

"What, even me?"

Jim laughed. "I don't own you, my crested friend. You're free to fly off any time you like. Although it would fairly break my heart if you did."

Doris smiled broadly. "Really?"

"Of course. You're quite indispensable, you know that. Who else would read the hieroglyphs for me?"

"Jim?"

"Yes?"

"Would you still like me if I were a poodle?"

He thought for a moment. "Yes, I suppose I would. But I prefer you as you are now. I've grown accustomed

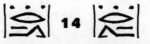

to your plumosity."

At this she smiled even more broadly, until her beak flapped up into her face with a loud thwaaaaang, and her jaw locked. "Jmmmmmm—"

"What is it?"

"I'v dn t agn. Cn y gv m a hnd pls?"

Jim reached up and, with one swift pull, flicked her beak downwards as he always had to do whenever Doris was feeling particularly happy with herself.

They had travelled slowly, for it was after all Sunday morning, and it is impossible to do anything in a hurry on a Sunday morning. At last they arrived in Gurna, where they went directly along the bustling main dirt road to the Amun-Ra Tea-rooms.

Brenda pulled up in front of their favourite establishment and Jim and Doris leapt off. As Jim tied Brenda to the camel-post, Mrs Amun-Ra came rushing out into the courtyard, dusting flour off her hands and tea-leaves from her hair.

"Ah, Mr Jim," she cried, "so good to see you again. You are looking very well. Welcome." She grasped both his cheeks between her thumbs and forefingers and flibbertigibbetted them with such warm fierceness that his eyes watered and his pith helmet fell off.

"Prrrreeeeaaaarrrrk!" prrrreeeeaaaarrrrked Doris.

"Oh, you be quiet, you jealous bird, you," beamed Mrs Amun-Ra. She was about to start on Doris's cheeks but the wary bird flew off to the perch Mrs Amun-Ra

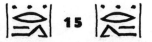

kept at their reserved table in the shadiest corner of the courtyard.

"How are you, Mrs A?" Cairo Jim asked as he picked up his hat.

"I am as fine as the sun is golden, Mr Jim. Come, come, your table waits for you like the Sphinx waits for its sweetheart."

She led him to the table. Doris was pacing anxiously up and down the perch. "You be patient, Miss Doris. I have your favourites hot from the oven. The snails are plump and luscious this week. The usual for you, Mr Jim?"

"Yes please. And a plate of worms for the camel."

"No problem." And off she bustled into the kitchen.

When she had brought Doris her shergold snail cakes and Brenda her worms and Jim his usual – shergold cakes (minus snails) and a pot of hot black tea with slices of lemon – she sat with Jim and wiped the back of her neck with the hem of her apron. "Well," she breathed heavily, "how is the finding of Martenarten happening?"

"Slowly, Mrs A," said Jim between mouthfuls. "Very slowly."

"About as slowly as the sands of time, perhaps?"

"Even slower I'm afraid. We dig away day after day, sometimes long into the night, but nothing much turns up. Although yesterday I found a picture of Edith Sitwell lying on top of my shovel."

Mrs Amun-Ra looked puzzled. "Tell me, Mr Jim,

why would someone take a picture of Edith Sitwell lying on top of your shovel?"

"No, I'm sorry, the picture *itself* was lying on top of my shovel."

"Ah."

"It must have blown in during the night."

"This Edith Sitwell, she was a poet, yes?"

Jim sipped his tea. "That's right. When I was younger she was one of my favourites. She helped inspire me to become a poet myself. Although it doesn't pay of course."

"You have the picture with you?"

"No, I've pinned it up in the tent next to Buzz Aldrin."

"I didn't know *he* was in town."

"No, his photograph. We found that in the dig last week."

"Oh, good. I'd have upset become if he was here and hadn't bothered to call in to see me. He usually does, you know."

Doris was enjoying her cakes immensely. "You've excelled this week, Mrs Amun-Ra," she screeched.

"Thank you, my little friend." She turned once again to Jim. "And so, Miss Jocelyn is no longer here?"

Cairo Jim shook his head. "Morocco," he said. "For a while."

Mrs Amun-Ra clasped her hands behind her head and stared into the skies. "It must be so exciting to be a flying person," she sighed. "All those different places

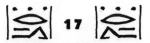

where they go, all those exotic people to meet. Ah me." She leaned closer. "Tell me, Mr Jim – you like Miss Jocelyn, yes?"

"Yes, she's a good mate."

"I notice you always a shave have when she's here."

"Hrrmph," Doris hrrmphed quietly.

"Yes," said Jim. "One has to maintain standards."

"And Miss Jocelyn, does she you like?"

"I suppose so. She usually brings Doris and Brenda and me little gifts. And she keeps coming back. So I suppose she does, yes."

Mrs Amun-Ra whispered secretively. "So when will we hear the pitter patter of little wedding bells?" Jim nearly choked on his shergold cake, while Doris almost fell off her perch.

"Er – well," he stammered, "to tell you the truth, Mrs A, I've never really thought about things like that. I'm an archaeologist as you know, and archaeologists have lots of things to keep themselves occupied."

Mrs Amun-Ra patted him on the hand. "But one night the day will come when things will different be," she smiled, "and then I think you should pop the cork to Miss Jocelyn. You will no better find. Take my word for it, me I understand these things."

Jim took a huge gulp of his tea. "Thank you, Mrs A. If ever I do decide to marry, you shall be the second to know."

"The second? Who will first be?"

He gave Doris a wink, to which she reearked.

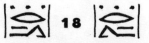

"Oh, I see," Mrs Amun-Ra laughed. "Well, I leave you now to your luncheon. Enjoy." She got up and went to attend to some other customers.

Not two minutes later they were joined by Miss Pyrella Frith, a very talented archaeological photographer whose services Cairo Jim had employed more than once. She had run all the way from the ferry and was breathless and excited as she flopped into the chair Mrs Amun-Ra had vacated. "Oh, Jim, I'm so glad I've found you," she gasped. "Oh my, it's hot, what do you think?"

"It's not too bad," he replied, watching her as she undid the long white ribbon which held her mosquito-netted, large-brimmed white straw hat onto her head. She took off the hat and placed it in the lap of her white skirt.

Miss Pyrella Frith always wore white. White skirts, white long-sleeved blouses, white boots that buttoned right up past her white ankles and, when the weather was cooler, long white gloves which she removed whenever she took photos. She was allergic to a great many things, the worst of which were the sun – she always covered herself with copious amounts of sunscreen lotion – and the savage mosquitoes that thrived and multiplied by the banks of the Nile. The North Pole had been her home for many years and she had learnt much about her profession from living in an igloo with a kindly Eskimo family who were photographically minded.

"Not too bad? Not too bad? My, it's hotter than a

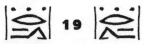 **19**

month of Sundays in Zanzibar." She slung her collapsible camera off her shoulder and onto Jim's table. "What I'd give to see snow again."

"Care for some tea?" asked Jim.

"Just the thing to quench a thirst like mine," she puffed. Without any further encouragement she took Jim's cup from its saucer and poured the hot tea down her throat. "That's much better," she said. "I needed that."

"There's nothing like Mrs A's brew," said Jim.

Pyrella shook out her long blonde hair and looked earnestly at Jim with her iceberg-blue eyes. "Now look," she breathed quickly, "I won't beat about the oasis, there's something very important I have to tell you."

"Oh, yes?"

"Yes. Now listen. Do you know the Rhampsinites twins?"

"Abdullah and Kelvin?"

"Yes. Sly creatures I know, but— *Yow!*" She jumped into the air.

Mrs Amun-Ra came running from the kitchen. "What is matter? Miss Pyrella, are you all right? What happened?"

Miss Pyrella Frith took a deep breath and sat down again. "So sorry for the disturbance, Mrs Amun-Ra. The tea was a bit hot."

"You should drink more slowly, perhaps?"

"May we have another cup please, Mrs A?" asked Jim.

"For you, Mr Jim, anything." And off she went

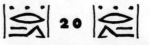 20

to get one.

"Now, as I was saying," continued Pyrella. "I've just caught the ferry over from Luxor. Not the best of rides this morning. I had to share my bench with a donkey who had very bad breath – goodness knows what he'd had for breakfast – but still, at least I'm here."

Reaching into her skirt pocket, she took out a white linen handkerchief with its corners tied around a small nuggetty object. She laid this bundle on the table and untied the knot as Mrs Amun-Ra returned with another cup and saucer. "I think this may be to your advantage," Pyrella said.

As she opened out the handkerchief, Jim's eyes widened and Doris's beak dropped open. Mrs Amun-Ra peered curiously at the tiny lapis lazuli brooch lying in the centre of the cloth.

For nearly a full minute, nobody said a word. Miss Pyrella Frith slapped a mosquito from her shin and sat back, crossing her arms and smiling smugly. She was obviously pleased with the reactions.

Then Jim spoke in a far-away voice. "Where did you get it?"

"From Kelvin Rhampsinites," said Pyrella. "Or was it Abdullah? I can never tell them apart. Anyway, one of them sold it to me outside the Winter Palace Hotel. Normally I never even look at what they're trying to flog. Most of their so-called artefacts are the most obvious reproductions – I mean, who ever heard of plastic scarabs? – but this looked different. There was something about this that seemed authentic. Ancient. So I bought it."

Cairo Jim's heart started to beat very quickly. "You've done well, Miss Frith." He picked up the brooch while Doris hopped over onto his shoulder. "Do you know what this is, Mrs A?" he asked.

Mrs Amun-Ra studied it as he held it up to the sun.

"No, Mr Jim, I'm afraid I do not."

"Ta," said Jim.

"That's quite all right," said Mrs Amun-Ra, putting the cup and saucer onto the table.

"No, I mean the carving on the brooch is Ta, the ancient Egyptian symbol for the moon."

"Ta," crooned Doris, her feathers stirring.

"And do you know what that means?"

Pyrella smiled and arched an eyebrow. She had something of an idea. "Martenarten perhaps?" she asked.

"Exactly. Ta is also the sign Pharaoh Martenarten adopted for himself when he did away with all the other gods and decreed that only the moon was to be worshipped. It made him none too popular with the High Priests at the time, I can tell you. They had to spend a fortune redecorating all the temples, and silver moon-paint was never cheap, not even in those days. But it wasn't only the temples. Martenarten ordered huge statues to be carved, massive figures of himself worshipping the moon, and these were erected everywhere the eye could see, in long lines stretching away into the desert, and sometimes even farther.

22

Masses of jewellery and anthracite vases and all sorts of fine things were produced, all of them in some way or other depicting Ta and Martenarten."

"My goodness me," gasped Mrs Amun-Ra.

"Yes, Mrs A, but unfortunately for us hardly any of these things have survived."

"Why is this?"

"After Pharaoh Martenarten was laid to rest, the High Priests, who had been reduced to a state of poverty because of the escalating price of silver moon-paint, went on a spree of destruction. They smashed all the statues' heads off and collected as many Martenarten things as they could find. These were then loaded onto a barge and set adrift into the Red Sea, never to be seen again. Legend has it the barge was blown up with explosives far out to sea. But now," and here Cairo Jim wiped away a tear of excitement that had escaped from behind his desert sun-spectacles, "now, thanks to Miss Frith, we are once again on the road to discovery."

"Well, throw me in the Nile and call me a felucca," said Mrs Amun-Ra.

"Was I right, Jim?" Pyrella asked. "Is it authentic?"

From the pocket of his extra-wide Sahara shorts Jim took a jeweller's small spyglass eyepiece. "Here's the expert," he said, and held it against Doris's eye. She squinted at the brooch.

"Rark, yes," she said after some scrutiny. "No doubt about it, it's the real McCoy all right."

"How can you tell?" asked Mrs Amun-Ra.

"The hieroglyphs," said Doris. "If you look carefully, you can just make them out with the naked eye. Through this, they're very clear. Prerak."

"Let me have a look," Jim said, taking the eyepiece from her. "Ah, yes, I see. All around the edge. How astonishing."

"What do they say?" asked Pyrella.

"Going clockwise," said Doris, "there's a moon, then two suns – they were called 'Ra' – followed by a small sign of an explosion which I'd say represents the destructive acts perpetrated by the High Priests. Then up near the top again we find a small duck, which was the symbol for the letter 'D' and finally the sign of Ay, the tutor who became Tutankhamun's successor."

"Ta Ra Ra Boom De Ay," whispered Jim.

"Exactly," said Doris. "Ta Ra Ra Boom De Ay."

"How jolly!" exclaimed Mrs Amun-Ra.

Jim turned to Pyrella. "Miss Frith, would you mind if I borrowed this for the day? There are a few questions I'd like to ask those Rhampsinites twins."

Pyrella poured herself some tea. "Keep it," she said. "A memento. And hopefully an omen of things to come."

"Why, thank you," he said, quite touched by her generosity. "How can I possibly repay you?"

"By employing me to do the photos the minute you make the discovery. I need the work, you know. There's nothing much archaeological happening at the moment, and I'm sick to death of shooting tourists stuffing their

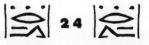

24

faces with ice-cream and tabouli."

"Of course I will, it was always my intention. There's none better than you, Miss Frith." He stood and handed Mrs Amun-Ra five Egyptian pounds. "Thank you, Mrs A," he said.

"Are already you going? You have not yet finished your shergolds."

"We'll eat them on the ferry. Come on, Doris."

"Wait, I get your change, Mr Jim."

"No, Mrs A, you keep it."

"Oh," said Mrs Amun-Ra, her pride wounded slightly.

Jim realised his mistake. "It's not baksheesh, my dear Mrs A. Use it to buy something nice for yourself. Perhaps a new hat or a roddle holder or something.

I would've bought something for you, but we've been flat out with the dig."

"Oh, well in that case—" She put the money in her apron pocket. "I'll get you a napkin to wrap around your shergolds. That way they'll stay nice and warm."

While she was off hunting for the napkin, Doris flew across and untethered Brenda, who was always more than content after having worms. Jim extended his hand to Pyrella. "You've been marvellous," he said.

"Not at all," said Miss Pyrella Frith, shaking Jim's hand vigorously. "Good luck."

"I think," said Jim, putting on his pith helmet and adjusting his elastic sock-garters, "that we have today crossed the path of luck and are now standing on the threshold of unimaginable opportunity." As he adjusted his hat, he thought for a moment about what he'd just said, then told Pyrella, "That'd make the beginning of a nice poem, what do you think?"

"I'd stick to archaeology if I were you," she said kindly.

"Here, Mr Jim, I've wrapped some, fresh from the kitchen. As hot as Horus they are, so don't scoff them for a little while."

"Thank you, Mrs A, you're a champion. We'll see you next week, the usual time."

Mrs Amun-Ra flibbertigibbetted his cheeks again, causing his ears to go red and tingle. "I hope you reach your goalposts this afternoon," she said. "Now off you go."

"Bye, Jim," Pyrella said. "Don't let them rip you off. You know what scoundrels they can be."

"I'll manage. It takes a cleverer villain than the Rhampsinites twins put together to pull the wool over Cairo Jim's eyes. Bye, all."

But as they hurriedly left the crowded courtyard of Mrs Amun-Ra's tea-rooms, they did not notice the plump, bearded, scowling stranger with the burgundy-coloured fez who was sitting in the opposite corner beneath a thirsty palm tree.

Neither the stranger nor his raven seemed very pleased at all.

3

AT THE SCARAB PIT OF THE RHAMPSINITES TWINS

"I AM SORRY, Cairo Jim, but you cannot bring your camel onto the ferry"

"Look," said Jim to the stubborn ferryman, "you don't seem to understand. It is absolutely imperative that we get over to Luxor in the quickest possible time. Our destiny awaits us. There is something of the utmost importance that we have to find out. So please, be a sport and let us on?"

"You can go on and your Doris can go on—"

"I'm not *his* Doris," screeched Doris, "I'm *my* Doris."

"—but the camel stays here. It is company policy."

Jim was becoming desperate; he had to get to the Rhampsinites brothers as soon as was humanly possible. His mind ticked over, then he said, "But you're mistaken, Mr Ferryman. This is no camel. This is a donkey."

The ferryman squinted suspiciously. "What do you think I am, an idiot?"

"Oh, no, the thought would never enter my mind. But the fact remains that this is my trusty donkey Deirdre who has accompanied Doris and myself through many an adventure. I'm surprised you haven't heard of her, her photo's been in the paper many times. Deirdre the Wonder Donkey?"

"No," said the ferryman, shaking his head. "I haven't."

"Say hello to the intelligent ferryman, Deirdre." Brenda, being the true Wonder Camel she was, brayed loudly in the best donkey tradition.

The ferryman walked slowly around the animal, inspecting every part of her. When he arrived back at her face, he looked up at Jim and Doris sitting high in the saddle.

"Okay, you tell me this, Cairo Jim: if she is a donkey, why is she so tall?"

"Being an Emnobellian Jungle Donkey accounts for that," said Jim. "They have to be tall, otherwise they're too short."

Doris started flapping her wings as she sat atop Jim's bleached helmet. "Hurry, Jim," she prowked under the noise of the flapping, "we've got to get a move on. The ferry's about to leave."

"That may be so," the ferryman said, walking alongside Brenda. "But how do you explain this?" He ran his ferry stick along Brenda's more prominent hump. "Donkeys, even those from the Emnobellian jungles, do not have these, surely?"

Jim looked down at the ferryman. "Not normally, no," he said quickly, "most Emnobellian Jungle Donkeys are flat-backed. Deirdre was too, until last

Thursday, when all of a sudden and with no warning she started to swell. Up and up and up she came until she reached this present state of swollenness."

"But why?" asked the ferryman.

"Mumps," said Cairo Jim.

"Mumps?"

"Mumps of the worst kind. In an Emnobellian Jungle Donkey, they distort the appearance so much the beast is often mistaken for a camel. Apart from this there are no dangerous effects, and the swelling usually goes down after a couple of weeks. But humans, on the other hand—"

"Yes?" the ferryman asked nervously. "What about humans?"

Jim leaned close and spoke very precisely. "If human beings are unfortunate enough to fall prey to Emnobellian Jungle Donkey Mumps, their eyes will puff up and their arms and legs will swell until they can no longer stand up or sit down or tie their sandal straps."

The ferryman began to turn green.

"Of course," Jim went on, keeping his eye on the nearly full ferry, "Doris and myself are not in a high-risk category. I spent several months in the jungles of Emnobellia some years ago and developed a resistance to diseases of this sort, and everyone knows a macaw cannot catch Emnobellian Jungle Donkey Mumps—"

"How *does* one catch it?" panicked the ferryman.

"Oh," said Jim, "any number of ways – kissing an Emnobellian Jungle Donkey is the most common—"

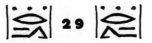

"Ha! There's no danger of that happening. Why for one thing, I don't even find her attra—"

"Mmmmmwwwwaaaa!" Brenda planted the slobberiest kiss full on his lips.

The ferryman threw up his hands in terror and, hitching up his galabiyya, jumped off the ferry ramp and raced willy-nilly along the road, spitting onto the ground and leaving a long trail of wispy dust behind him.

"Good work, Brenda," said Jim. "I was hoping that would happen. Such an awful lot of work to get onto a ferry, though."

"Come on," Doris crowed impatiently, "or they'll leave without us."

And so the three intrepid discoverers boarded the crowded ferry.

The Nile was calm and sparkling as the ferry steamed slowly to the East bank. Cairo Jim gave Doris a shergold cake and she munched happily, being careful not to drop any crumbs onto his hat. He could not eat anything now – he was far too excited about the potential information he was hoping to gain from the Rhampsinites brothers.

Many small feluccas sailed past, their sails full-blown in the steady breeze.

Gradually Luxor Temple loomed larger and larger in their sights as the ferry sludged closer to its destination, and before it had docked completely at the small wharf below the Temple, the trio jumped off and galloped

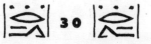

along the street towards the Winter Palace Hotel.

They galloped all the way into the lobby of the grand building and came to a skidding halt at the reception desk.

"Can I help you?" asked the man behind the desk.

"I hope so," said Jim, looking down at him from the saddle. "I was told the Rhampsinites brothers were here."

"Yes, this morning," the man said, eyeing Brenda anxiously. "They were selling their awful souvenirs to the tourists outside. But I told them to move on. They bring down the tone, you understand."

"I'm not at all surprised. Do you know where they went? It's extremely important we find them."

The receptionist was looking at Brenda as he spoke. "I suggest you try their scarab pit up the road. That's where they usually hang out."

"Thank you," said Jim. "I will."

He turned Brenda around and started to leave when the receptionist called after him. "I'd get that donkey seen to if I were you," he shouted. "I think she has mumps."

Brenda brayed noisily as they hurtled out into the sunshine.

At the scarab pit of the Rhampsinites twins, Abdullah Rhampsinites was busy hitting Kelvin Rhampsinites over the head with a plastic imitation canopic jar. "You fool, you scatterbrained, bungling fool!" he shouted.

"Ow! Stop hitting me," whined Kelvin.

"I'll stop hitting you when you realise what an absolute walking blunderer you are."

"Yowch! No, please, I realise, I realise."

"Blunderer, blunderer, blunderer!"

"Oooh, oooh, oooh! Mercy, mercy!"

"How could you have done it? That brooch was the only genuine thing we've ever had. Why did you sell it?"

"Ouch! I didn't mean to. It was a mistake. I got confused when she started haggling. I thought it was one of our fakes."

"We could have got a fortune for it at the Cairo Museum. Do you have any idea how rare Martenarten pieces are? They would have paid thousands. Idiot!"

"Ouch!"

"I could have bought Mother that perfume shop she's always dreamed about, with velvet lounges and satin cushions and a little picket camel-post out the front and lotus flowers everywhere—"

"And mood lighting," said Kelvin, "don't forget the mood lighting."

"And mood lighting," snarled Abdullah. "Blunderer!"

"Ooooh!"

Abdullah paused briefly to get his breath back. "But even if I could buy it for her, it wouldn't do any good," he said. "She'd probably think it was from you."

"It's not my fault she can't tell us apart. Nobody can."

"But she's our own mother, for goodness' sake!"

"Yaaaargh!"

"Tell me who bought the brooch, blunderer."

"It was that photographer who's always dressed in white. The one with the mosquito net."

"Pyrella Frith," seethed Abdullah.

"That's her," Kelvin said. "She gave me three pounds for it."

At this, Abdullah's fury increased even further. "Three pounds? Three pounds? How many satin cushions do you think I could buy for three pounds? You pathetic blu—"

"Drop that fake canopic jar!" a voice boomed from above.

Abdullah jumped and dropped the jar onto Kelvin's head.

"Oww!" cried Kelvin.

They looked up and saw the figures of Jim, Doris and Brenda silhouetted against the brightness of the noonday sun.

"It's Cairo Jim," whispered Kelvin, as the three descended the narrow path into the scarab pit. "What does he want?"

"How should I know? He may want some scarabs. Get up and fetch the wheelbarrow."

"I can't, you're kneeling on my chest."

"Fool." Abdullah stood and then stepped off his brother. Kelvin raced away to the dilapidated tin shed where they kept the barrow.

"Why, if it isn't Kelvin Rhampsinites," said Jim as he jumped off Brenda.

"That's right, Cairo Jim," said the Rhampsinites twin, "it isn't. I am Abdullah."

"I'm sorry."

"No, don't be. It is a far, far better thing to be Abdullah than to be Kelvin. At least I have a brain."

"And a scheming one at that," thought Doris as she flew from Jim's helmet and perched on top of Abdullah's head.

"Get off, you feathered thing, you," squealed Abdullah, trying to swipe at Doris with his bony hand. She screeched and flew to Brenda, where she took refuge between the Wonder Camel's humps.

Kelvin trundled his squeaky wheelbarrow, full to the brim with shiny plastic scarabs, over to his brother. "Cairo Jim," he whined, "we are pleased to see you. Maybe you would like to buy some scarabs? A gross perhaps? We have a sale on at the moment and would be—"

"Put them away," said Jim. "You know I have no interest in your hoodwinking activities."

The brothers looked at each other and sniggered. They loved being complimented in such a way.

Brenda regarded them through narrow eyes as they stood side by side. It was the first time she had seen the twins close-up and she was amazed at how identical they were. They were both very tall and thin as sticks. Both wore matching black-and-red striped galabiyyas and bright green plastic sandals which they had made for themselves in their small workshed at the back of the pit. It was here they also produced the thousands of plastic scarabs and fake canopic jars which they flogged to unsuspecting tourists, claiming they were valuable finds from the nineteenth dynasty. The twins had black eyepatches, which they had worn since childhood, over their left eyes, but nobody knew why, and nobody had ever bothered to find out. Their hair was cut bristly short and was always dirty, and between them, they only had seven teeth. These were yellow and grotty.

"I am here," continued Jim, "on a matter of far greater importance." He took the brooch from his shirt pocket and held it out in front of them. "I need to know where you found this."

Abdullah's eye bulged as he looked at his lost treasure once again. He frowned a grotty frown and thumped his brother on the arm.

"Ouch," moaned Kelvin.

"Cut it out, you brutish man," warned Jim, "and tell me."

Abdullah Rhampsinites's frown melted upwards across his face into an ingratiating leer. "Ah, Cairo Jim," he said, as though Jim was his best and most valued mate, "that worthless piece of junk? You don't want *that*, I'm sure. Let me take it off your hands."

He put his hand into a slit in his galabiyya – Doris went on full alert at this – and took out a handful of grimy, crumpled money. When Doris saw it was only money he had extricated and not a dagger or gun or some other kind of weapon, her feathers relaxed slightly, but she still kept a careful eye.

"Would you perhaps like to sell it to me?" asked Abdullah. "I'll make you a very generous offer for it. One you can't refuse. How about a pound?"

"Don't be ridiculous," said Jim.

"Okay, one-and-a-half pounds?"

"You're trying my patience—"

"All right, my final offer: two pounds and as many scarabs as you can carry."

"This brooch is not for sale," Jim said defiantly.

Abdullah frowned again. "You sure?" he asked glumly.

"Positive."

"Not even if I throw in two pairs of sandals for the donkey?"

Brenda snorted loudly.

"I'm sorry, for the camel?"

"Not on your Nellie," said Cairo Jim.

"Leave Mother out of this," Kelvin said.

Jim put the brooch back into his pocket and took a step closer to the two. "Now look, Abdullah—"

"I'm Kelvin."

"Now look, Kelvin, I haven't got all day. Where did this come from?"

"Information like that does not come cheaply," growled Abdullah.

Jim sighed and pulled out his wallet. "Perhaps this will help lubricate that heinous tongue of yours. But I want the truth." He held out a pound note.

"Ah, now you're talking, Cairo Jim." Abdullah snatched the note from Jim's hand, feeling flattered that his tongue had been described as heinous. Although he had no idea what it meant, the word sounded appropriate in a dastardly sort of way.

"Well?" asked Jim.

"I found it," said Kelvin.

"Obviously," Jim said. "Obviously you found it. What I want to know is, *where*?"

Abdullah held out his hand. "More information, more baksheesh," he leered.

Jim sighed and handed over another pound note.

"In the sand," Kelvin whined.

"There is sand everywhere in Egypt," said Jim, his voice becoming thin. "Where exactly in the sand?" Out came Abdullah's hand again, and into it Jim put another pound.

"In the Valley of the Kings."

Jim glanced across at Doris and she flapped her wings. This was what they were hoping to hear. "Whereabouts in the Valley?"

Another pound.

"Near some of the tombs."

"Which tombs?" Jim's throat was becoming dry with anticipation. He handed over the pound.

Kelvin was about to answer, but Abdullah interrupted. "My brother's memory is not very good in the afternoon—"

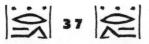

"Yes it is," protested Kelvin.

"Bite your tongue!"

"But it is."

Abdullah thumped Kelvin on the arm and turned to Jim. "He tends to forget things, especially when the sun is beating down so hard on his head. What he needs is a hat to protect him."

"A hat, eh?" asked Jim.

"And hats do not come cheaply, my friend."

Cairo Jim flicked through his money until his thumb came to the bigger denominations. He tugged out a five-pound note. "This should cover it."

Abdullah laughed, opening his mouth wide and revealing his four awful teeth. "Ah, Cairo Jim, that is quite decent of you, quite decent indeed, but I am afraid five pounds will not buy a very protective hat. Why, the brim would scarcely cover his ears. You wouldn't want my dear brother to have sunburnt ears now, would you?"

"Perish the thought," Jim said through gritted teeth. "Here's ten."

"Oh, what a good man you are. So very generous and caring." Abdullah took the money. "But the kind of hat my brother needs is one with a little solar-powered propeller on the top, so when the sun is extremely harsh the little propeller spins around and cools his hair. There is nothing worse than sweaty hair on the back of the neck—"

"All right, all right. Here. Take twenty."

"Thirty."

"Twenty-five."

"Twenty-nine."

"Twenty-six."

"Twenty-eight."

"Twenty-seven."

"Twenty-seven-and-a-half."

"Twenty-seven pounds, and not a piastre more." Jim quickly counted the money out and threw it at Abdullah's feet. "Now tell me," he said, his voice rising as Abdullah scrambled to pick up the notes, "near which tombs did you find the brooch?"

"A fly whisk would be nice too," suggested Kelvin. "One made from the tail of the zebra. They are not cheap either—"

"If you don't tell me this very instant, you thieving scoundrels—"

"Why, thank you, Cairo Jim," said Abdullah.

"—I'll set Doris on to both of you. Doris!" The great plumed bird flew over and came to rest upon Jim's crooked arm. She eyed the twins threateningly.

"Heaven forbid!" wailed Abdullah, full of fear at the thought of all those feathers fluttering about his head. "Tell him, tell him," he urged his brother.

"I found it between the tombs of Thutmose I and Seti II," blurted Kelvin. "Off the path where nobody goes."

"Near the small hill shaped like a battered trilby hat?" asked Jim.

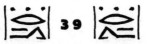

"Yes, near that very hill."

"Fleeeerrrrk," fleeeerrrrked Doris happily. "And it was just lying in the sand?"

"Just lying there," Kelvin whined.

"*On* the sand or buried?"

"Buried a little way down."

"But how did you know it was there?"

Kelvin shuddered. "Because of the raven," he said. "A huge black thing with red eyes and a rough yellow tongue and feathers—"

"Yeergh," said Abdullah.

"—feathers as black as pitch. If it had not swooped on me, forcing me to fall to the ground and bury my face beneath my arms, I would never have found the brooch. I hate birds as much as my brother does, their feathers give me the most ugly rash, little red spots everywhere. So I lay there, as still as I could. As still as the Nile on a windless night, until the rotten thing flew away. When I opened my eye, I thought there was something strange about the sand underneath my nose. It was not soft like everywhere else, there was something hard about it. I dared not move in case the raven came back, so very gently I wiggled my nose until all the sand beneath it was brushed away. And there it was, that beautiful thing, its hieroglyphs pressed close to my hooter."

Cairo Jim was elated. He was so elated he could feel a full symphony orchestra swelling in his heart, a mighty stirring that all at once rose up and smothered all the

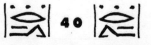

doubts he had been having about the dig. Now, after hearing Kelvin's story, he knew he was searching in the right place. With Doris still on his arm he bounded up onto Brenda's bigger hump and swung the Wonder Camel in the direction of the path.

"Thank you, Abdullah," Jim cried as Brenda clambered quickly up and out of the scarab pit. "You've been invaluable."

"But I am Kelvin!"

"And a blundering one at that," Abdullah seethed, thumping him hard on the arm.

"But Jim, what about our swim?" Doris asked as they galloped back to the ferry.

"I'm afraid that'll have to wait, my dear," said Jim, his eyes ablaze with fresh enthusiasm. "We must move while time is still on our side. Do you know what this means? This one little brooch holds the key to our destiny. We are, after all this time, on the right trail. Whacko!"

"Whacko," said Doris, a little bit miffed that she'd be missing out on her dip in the Nile, but happy nonetheless because of Jim's excitement. He seldom said "Whacko".

Brenda, too, was excited as she half-galloped, half-danced from Gurna village back to their lonely camp in the Valley.

There, as the sun sank in a warm glow behind the hill shaped like a battered trilby hat, Cairo Jim dug and dug,

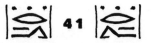

filling bucket upon bucket with rocks, sand and stone. Doris carted each bucketload to the rock pile and emptied it obediently, while Brenda kept an ever-alert vigil over the scene.

With each rock and every grain of sand he removed, Cairo Jim's heart beat quicker as he imagined the unspeakable treasures awaiting them deep in the earth.

They were totally unaware of the long brass telescope which had been spying upon them from across the Valley for the last three weeks.

4

MEANWHILE, OVER THE SANDHILLS AND NOT TOO FAR AWAY

THE TELESCOPE was still focused on them when Cairo Jim, Doris and Brenda, all very weary from their labours, decided to head back to their camp for a few hours of cool sleep.

The raven with the throbbing red eyes and rough yellow tongue and feathers as black as pitch turned her attention from the eyepiece to her master. "They've left the dig," she croaked. "They're all going back to the tent."

The plump, bearded man in the burgundy fez pulled out his pocket-watch from his emerald-green waistcoat and looked at it in the moonlight. "Eleven thirty-three," he said quietly. "They've been at it late tonight. Hmm."

Desdemona the raven gurgled into the still night air.

"How big is the rock pile?" the man asked anxiously.

She looked through the telescope again. "Much bigger, much, much, bigger."

"Let me see." He got out of the wicker chair where he had been listening to dirge-like music playing on his antique gramophone and went to the telescope.

"Ah, yes," murmured Captain Neptune Bone, bending to look through it. "It's almost big enough.

A couple more days and we should be ready."

"Ready to plant the explosives?" asked Desdemona.

"Arrrr," sneered Bone, who had seen far too many pirate movies when he was a small child. "Ready to plant the explosives."

Desdemona hopped up and down excitedly. "Bang, crash, ratso for Cairo Jim. Nevermore, nevermore, nevermore!"

Bone returned to his chair and lowered himself slowly into it. "Ah, rapscallion," he said to the glossy bird, "this is my most ingenious plan to date. There is still much to be done, but when we have driven Cairo Jim and his little menagerie from the Valley, Martenarten and all his goodies will be mine. Mine. *Mine!*" He threw back his head and laughed.

Desdemona pecked a flea from her wing and spat it onto the sand. "So he's on the right track then?" Bone fixed her with a rude stare. "Of course he's on the right track, you stupid flying thing. Do you think we'd be down here watching his every move if he weren't?"

"But you told them in Cairo—"

"I told the Old Relics Society that he was digging in the wrong place, to undermine their confidence in him."

"But why?"

Bone sighed. "Sometimes you are very thick for a raven. Because then word would get back to Gerald Perry Esquire, and he would withdraw all his funding. Then there'd be no way Cairo Jim's work could continue. Unfortunately, Perry has more faith in Jim than I thought. That's why we're here…"

"Oh," croaked the bird.

Bone locked his fleshy fingers together and stretched his arms towards the stars until his knuckles cracked loudly.

"Aaaaaaar," Desdemona shrieked. "I wish you wouldn't do that. You know it makes my eyes throb harder."

"Martenarten, Martenarten, Martenarten," mused Bone. "The lost Pharaoh. But not for long. Soon the discovery of Martenarten and the name of Neptune Bone will be one and the same. I will go down in history as the man who uncovered it all. And do you know what will please me most?"

"What might that be?"

"That Cairo Jim will have nothing to do with it. Nothing whatsoever. He will be forgotten, seen as the man who gave up and walked away. Or rather, *ran* away, if my scheme goes true to plan."

"There's one thing I don't understand," said Desdemona as she pecked at the feathers on her back for more fleas.

"What don't you understand, you scatterbrained scavenger?"

"What good will it be to blow up the rock pile? Surely it'd be better if we exploded the place where they're digging?"

"Idiot bird," Bone smiled. "Think about it. If we blew up their dig, there's a real danger we might also

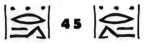

damage the Tomb. I have a strong feeling Jim is very close to the entrance. No, I've worked it out carefully. We set the explosives at the bottom of the rock pile, then when the big bang comes, the whole lot – stones, rocks, rubble and all – will go crashing down the hill towards the dig. The entrance will be buried deeply, and all their months of work will have been an absolute waste. Arrr."

"And then? Then what?"

"If I know Cairo Jim – and I used to very well, remember – he will be discouraged, but not ready to give up. The stubborn archaeologist he is, he'll send a letter or telegram to Gerald Perry Esquire, telling him what has happened and asking for more time. But that will be impossible."

"Why?"

"Because more time means more money. Lots and lots more money, and I happen to know for a fact that Gerald Perry Esquire's funds are running out. Ever since he opened up that chain of take-away pigeon restaurants, things haven't been going at all well for him. He's depending on Cairo Jim's excavation, and the publicity it will bring, to boost business. So naturally, when he receives Cairo Jim's news, he'll reply that he can no longer afford it. And Jim, who can't possibly afford to continue the dig under his own steam, will be forced to leave."

Neptune Bone stretched his pudgy neck and ran the tips of his fingers through his ginger-brown beard.

"And that, my flea-ridden bag of feathers, is where I

step in. As soon as Jim and his friends have scrammed, I remove the rubble and continue where they left off."

Desdemona let out a huge raven laugh that pierced Bone's ears with its fingernails-on-the-blackboard noise.

"Arr, stop it, stop it," Bone pleaded, his hands trying to blot out the noise. "What's giving you so much mirth?"

The eyes of the raven throbbed mockingly. "There's something you haven't thought of, that's what," she gloated.

"No there isn't."

"Yes there is."

"No there is *not*. I've thought of everything. You do when you're a genius like what I am."

"Genius, schemius. I tell you there is."

Bone's beard bristled in the still night air. "Okay, smartyfeathers," he snarled, "what is it?"

Desdemona lay back in the dust, folding her huge wings underneath the back of her head. "Well," she said smugly, "just exactly *how* are you planning to get rid of all the rubble? It took Jim and that gaudy Doris three months to clear all that. How long do you think it'll take us, especially with your being allergic to hard work?"

"I'm not allergic to hard work," grumbled Bone. "I just have sensitive hands. I get them from my mother."

"Well, with your sensitive hands, we'll be slogging away for a year at least."

Neptune Bone picked up a rock and, being careful not to chip any of his fingernails, lobbed it at the bird.

"Yaaaaaaar," she wailed as it clunked on her forehead.

"You underestimate me, Desdemona. I told you I'd thought of everything."

"All right," she moaned, rubbing her head, "then how do we clear it away?"

"With this." From his plus-fours trousers, Bone removed a fat wad of crisp money.

The raven sat bolt upright. "Where did you get all that?"

"You didn't think I gave *all* of our finds from the Principality of Purcellopania to the Cairo Museum, did you? Some of those precious pieces I sold privately. This is merely a small part of the profit."★

"You naughty archaeologist!"

"All I have to do is pop down into Gurna village and round up a couple-of-dozen strapping young men. It's surprising what a thousand pounds will buy. With that kind of help, we'll have the pile cleared in a week."

"Clever thinking," muttered Desdemona.

"So admit you were wrong."

"All right, all right," she scowled. "I was wrong."

"Arrr. Yet again. And admit I *am* a genius."

"You're a genius," she said under her breath.

"A what?"

★ Captain Neptune Bone is credited with discovering the existence of the Principality of Purcellopania, a long-obscure state where everyone rode themselves to distraction on the world's first bicycles.

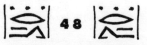

"A genius."

"I didn't hear you."

"A *genius*!"

"And don't you ever forget it."

Bone stood and strolled around his camp. "You see," he said softly, "it's all part of the master plan I have. Part Two is of equal importance: The Scaring of Cairo Jim. We can't just blow things up, out of the blue and for no apparent reason. Why, he'd suspect something, wouldn't he? So what we need is something to frighten him." He turned to his companion. "That's why you've been dropping those photographs into the dig. Which reminds me, it's time for the next."

He went to a large cedar chest outside the doorflap of his tent pavilion and lifted the lid. Inside, it was crammed with magnifying glasses, gramophone records, a collection of different coloured fezzes, photograph albums, assorted artefacts gathered from expeditions to Egypt, Peru, Sumatra and several of the smaller African countries, past editions of the Old Relics Society's newsletter, and an antique manicure kit in a tortoise-shell case, which he used every morning and evening without fail.

From one of the photograph albums he took a postcard. "Later tonight, bird, when all the lamps are out in Cairo Jim's camp, I want you to take this picture of William the Conqueror and drop it in the usual place."

"Why William the Conqueror?"

"Time will reveal all," he answered mysteriously.

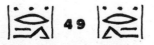

49

Desdemona stretched and yawned. "I feel peckish. How about some seaweed?"

Bone shuddered. "I couldn't think of anything worse."

"Suit yourself," she shrugged, and hopped over to the canvas bag where she kept her stash of tinned Japanese seaweed. From the top of the bag she rolled out the nearest tin and started to pierce it open with her beak.

"A cigar wouldn't go astray, though," thought Bone aloud. He entered his tent and started to rummage in the cupboard underneath his small bedside table. He found a thick brown cigar, bit off the end, spat it onto the ground, and lit the cigar with his silver cigar-lighter. Then he stepped out into the calm night and pondered.

There was still one small problem with his plan: when to plant the explosives. He couldn't do it at night; there was a danger that the light from their torches would be seen by Brenda the Wonder Camel, who slept very little.

As he took a long, slow puff on the evil-smelling tobacco, he realised what he needed was a daylight diversion. Something to get Jim, Doris and Brenda away from the dig for a couple of hours. But what?

He looked down at Desdemona, her beak pecking ferociously into the tin of seaweed. The slurping noises she made sent a shiver down his spine. He blew a thick column of smoke at her and walked to his telescope at the edge of camp.

What could he concoct to get them away? He took the telescope from its stand, raised it to his eye, and moved it across the Valley.

Slowly the blackened images of the night came into focus.

Then suddenly he saw something which gave him an idea. Something far away, down near the paddocks, lit only by the pale moonlight.

He clenched the cigar with his teeth as his lips curled into a smile. A plan began to take shape in his mind, a plan of the most deceitful kind. Just the thing to suck Cairo Jim in, he thought. He trembled at its naughtiness.

But in order for it to go ahead, he would need another pair of hands. Or better still, another two pairs of hands.

He replaced the telescope on its stand and went quickly to his portable writing desk inside the tent. From a drawer, he took a piece of faint yellow writing paper, printed on the top with his name and title, "Captain Neptune Bone, Archaeologist", followed by his emblem, a small drawing of a Purcellopanian bicycle. He found a felt-tipped pen in the drawer and scribbled a hurried note:

Dear Rhampsinites twins,

Meet me here at my camp tomorrow (Monday) at noon. I have a proposition which you may find interesting and profitable. Arrr.

(Signed) Captain N. Bone

P.S. If you can't find me, look for the raven in the sky. I will be directly beneath her.

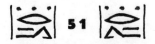

He folded the note and stuffed it into a lime-green envelope. "Desdemona!" he shouted. "Come here!"

"I haven't finished yet," she slurped.

"Right this instant, you preposterous predator!"

Desdemona kicked her near-empty tin aside and hopped to the door of the tent. "What is it now?" she asked as she picked at her beak with a claw.

"Give me your tongue."

"Oh, no, not again," she winced.

"Give it to me."

"No, not for *that*—"

"Don't be disobedient. Poke."

"Oh, please, do I really have to?"

"*Poke*!"

He reached out and grabbed the tip of her coarse, seaweed-coated tongue with his fingers, then ran the inside edge of the envelope flap up and down it four times.

"Yergh!" breathed the raven, trying with all her might to pull away.

He then let go and she went reeling backwards out of the tent, sprawling into a cloud of dust. Bone rose and followed her, the sealed envelope in his hand.

"Blecccch," spat Desdemona. "I hate stationery."

"You overreact fiercely sometimes. Now listen to me carefully." He puffed his cigar as he looked out over the Valley. "Everything is now dark in Cairo Jim's camp. The time is right for the delivery. But first I want you to take this to those Rhampsinites twins." He thrust the letter at her.

Desdemona's eyes throbbed and lit up. "Arrr," she drooled, "can I swoop them again? I almost got Kelvin the other week. Or was it Abdullah? I can never tell them apart—"

"No, you may not swoop them," said Bone, the cigar smoke curling through his beard. "We need their co-operation."

"Ratso," said Desdemona.

"So hurry, be off with you. There is much to be done."

Desdemona hopped up and down, "Much, much, much. Nevermore, nevermore, nevermore."

She stuffed the note into her beak and hopped over to her seaweed bag where she had left the postcard of William the Conqueror. Stuffing this also into her gob, she gave a feathered salute to the Captain, and took off into the sky with a muffled whoooooooooosh.

As she soared towards the stars, Neptune Bone went to the cluttered chest and took out his manicure kit. He selected a disc of dirgey music and wound the gramophone.

The machine shuddered and stirred into life, and he placed the needle onto the record. The low chords sank deeply into his head.

"Martenarten, Martenarten, Martenarten—"

His very heart pumped the name of the forgotten Pharaoh through his body as he buffed his fingernails fastidiously and stared out into the blackness of the night.

▲▲▲▲▲ 5 ▲▲▲▲▲

THE RETURN OF MEMNON

ON THURSDAY MORNING, Jim, Doris and Brenda took a break from the dig and were having morning tea on the picnic blanket Jocelyn Osgood had left for such occasions, when Doris stuck her beak into Jim's leather knapsack and pulled out her pack of cards.

"Anyone for a little hand?" she asked as she shuffled.

"No thanks, Doris," said Jim. "Not this morning, if you don't mind."

"Brenda'll be in it, won't you, Brenda?"

Before Brenda had a chance to snort, Doris started to deal out two hands. "Gin rummy," she told the Wonder Camel, who raised her eyelashes in despair.

Jim sipped his tea and sighed.

"What's up?" asked Doris, noticing his perplexed expression.

Jim didn't seem to hear her, so she let out a short, sharp screech, which made Brenda drop her cards onto the blanket.

"I'm sorry, Doris," said Jim, who had been a long way away. "Did you say something?"

"I asked what was up. You look worried."

Cairo Jim laughed and took off his pith helmet. "Ah, no, I'm not worried. Why should I be worried when we're on the verge of such a great opportunity?" He picked up the pot and poured more tea. "No, I'm just a little puzzled, that's all."

Doris put down her cards, just as Brenda had managed to pick up all of hers again and arrange them into a neat hoof-full. "Puzzled? By what?" she asked.

"By all those things we keep finding in the dig. All those photos and the like."

"I wouldn't worry about them too much if I were you," she said.

"But how peculiar that they keep popping up like that. Nearly every time we go away and come back, there's something new. And what an odd assortment of characters. First we found Buzz Aldrin, then Edith Sitwell, then last Sunday there was William the Conqueror on his horse, and yesterday Alice B. Toklas. Goodness, how strange."

"Who's Alice B. Toklas?"

Jim sipped his tea. "She was a writer, once upon a time. A good friend of another very well-known writer named Gertrude Stein."

"Ooh," crooned Doris. "Did they write adventure stories?"

"Not really, no."

"Pity. I'd love a good adventure story right now."

"What sort?"

She scratched her head with her wing. "Let me see," she began. "I know: something with jungles and snakes and things, and the hero looking for his sweetheart whom he's to find before the gang of sweaty rogues captures him and forces him to reveal the whereabouts of the Puce Empress, a priceless statue from China which has been missing for ninety years, but which the hero knows is buried in an abandoned mine somewhere in the mountains of Patagonia."

Doris had been doing little flying pirouettes above the blanket as she lost herself in her adventure. She came to land on Brenda's head with a flutter. Brenda pretended she wasn't there and concentrated on not spilling her tea.

"And how would it end, Doris?" asked Jim.

"Oh, there'd be a mighty swordfight between the hero and the gang of sweaty rogues, but the hero would win all right and his sweetheart, who looks exactly like Jocelyn Osgood, would fall into his arms and make him have a shave right then and there." She gave a brief scowl. "And then they'd do a tango or perhaps a rumba through the jungle, with the stars shining above them."

"And what about the Puce Empress? Would that be found?"

Doris stopped fluttering and thought for a moment. "No," she said firmly. "The Puce Empress would remain in the Patagonian mine, and the hero wouldn't want it any more because he's found his sweetheart at last, and that's enough for one story anyway."

"If it weren't for your imagination, I sometimes think I'd be quite lost," Jim said cheerfully.

Doris felt pleased with herself and smiled. A snatch

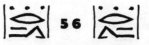

of a tune started to float into her head and she jumped off Brenda and flew high up towards the sun.

She remained suspended in the hot, cloudless sky for a minute, then plummeted down to the centre of the blanket, where she came to rest gracefully on her feet.

"And now for a little song," she announced.

Covering her beak with her wing, she gave a small cough. Then she clasped her wings in front of her and, with perfect macaw pitch, let the tune roll out:

Feathers,
I've got feathers,
and they flutter so that I can hardly speak
while we're digging for another lost antique,
but I'd rather be off dancing beak to beak.

She hummed a few bars at the end of it and accompanied them with an energetic tap-dancing display amidst the crockery. When she had finished, she stepped back and took a low bow.

Jim beamed and clapped while Brenda snorted an amused snort.

"Bravo, bravo. Your dulcet tones are an inspiration. What a clever bird!"

Doris's smile became dangerously broad. "Jmmmm—? Cn y flck my bk pls?"

"For you, my feathered diva, anything."

"Quaaaaooo," snorted Brenda excitedly, rising to her

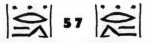

feet. She gestured with her head towards the dirt road on the crest of a nearby hill.

Jim also stood and Doris flew to his shoulder. Far off in the distance they could see a thin white figure pedalling furiously towards them on a white bicycle.

"Now who could that be?" wondered Jim. He quickly fetched his binoculars and looked once again. "Why, it's Miss Frith."

"What does she want?" squawked Doris.

"From her determined expression, I'd say she wants to tell us something. Her teeth are clenched very firmly and there is eagerness in her eyebrows. Doris, would you mind fetching another cup and saucer from my tent? She may need some refreshment upon her arrival."

Without a squawk, Doris did as she was asked.

Five minutes later, Miss Pyrella Frith arrived at the dig. In a cloud of dust and with a ring of her bell she brought her bicycle to a halt next to the picnic blanket and leapt off. Her teeth were clenched even more firmly now, because for the last five minutes she had been bumping along through the unpaved sandhills, and her bicycle seat was not well sprung.

"Hello, Jim, Doris, Brenda," she greeted them breathlessly as she took off her mosquito net and hat. "I'm glad I've caught you."

"Morning, Miss Frith," said Jim. "Would you like some tea?"

"There's no time, Jim."

"No time?"

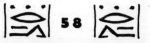

"No. There's something extraordinary about to happen down near Gurna, something you must come and hear."

"What is it?" asked Jim.

"I'm too puffed to tell you now. You must come with me straight away if we're to get a good position. I want to get some decent photos, and there's already quite a crowd there." She paused to flick a flea from her leg. "That's odd. I didn't know there were fleas in the Valley."

"A lot of odd things have been happening here lately," said Jim.

She fanned her face with her hat and took a deep breath. "Come, we must hurry. Believe me, this should be quite amazing."

"Righto then." He knew that Pyrella Frith did not make statements like that lightly, so he raced to the camp and grabbed Brenda's saddle.

"Shall I clear the tea things?" Doris asked him as he threw the saddle over Brenda's humps and strapped it firmly down.

"No time for that," Pyrella said. She put on her hat and net again and threw her leg over her bicycle. "Follow me, I know a shortcut."

Jim put on his pith helmet and hoisted himself up onto Brenda. "Leave them till we get back, Doris. But bring four oranges, we'll eat them on the way."

"Rightio." Doris scooped them up and joined Jim on the saddle.

"Miss Frith, I hope this won't take too long. We still have a lot of work to do."

Pyrella smiled as she started to pedal off. "I'm sure you won't be disappointed. It's something you wouldn't want to miss for quids."

"Gee-up, Brenda, my lovely." He gave her a gentle prod with his foot and she started to follow Pyrella's bicycle.

"Miss Frith, tell me one thing," he called. "Where are we going?"

"To the Colossi of Memnon," she answered without looking back.

"Arrrr, they're off at last," sneered Neptune Bone, his eye glued to the telescope.

"About time," grumbled Desdemona.

"Have you packed all the explosives into that bag yet?"

"Almost, almost. I've got dynamite, T.N.T., gelignite and gunpowder. There's only the nitroglycerine to go."

Bone turned to her. "Be extremely careful with that," he warned. "One slip of your wings and we'll both be paddling a felucca into the After Life a little sooner than we'd planned."

Carefully she dragged the bottle of nitroglycerine from the tent-pavilion and eased it into the bag. Bone returned to the telescope and watched Pyrella, Jim, Doris and Brenda weaving their way through the hills.

"And don't forget the shovel," he said.

"I haven't."

"And the small broom to brush away our footprints."

"It's here."

"And the air freshener to rid the air of your odour. We can't leave any lingering evidence."

"Fatso," she said under her breath.

"And when you've finished there, go and get me a new fez from the chest. I think I'll wear the tangerine one today."

"Lazy blob."

"And then go and fetch my driving gloves. The purple ones, to go with my spats."

"Would you like me to rinse your socks as well?" she seethed.

"No. That can wait until we get back."

"Chubby chops."

"But you can crank up the Bugatti for me. I don't want to get my hands grimy."

"Overdressed pincushion."

He hurled a stone at her, making sure it did not fall anywhere near the bag of explosives. His aim was good and it fell on her head.

"Youch!" she squealed at the sudden clunk. She looked up into the sky, trying to work out from where the stone had come.

"And in future, don't be so rude," growled Neptune Bone.

Miss Pyrella Frith had been right; a large crowd had filled the paddocks surrounding the Colossi of Memnon.

Many people had brought picnic lunches and had spread out on the grass. Tourists and local sightseers, all curious as to what was going to happen, were thronging to pay their admission money and find a good position in front of the ancient statues. Anticipation filled the air.

Pyrella brought her bicycle to a stop and waited for Brenda to catch up. She took her Voigtlander camera from its bag on her bicycle rack. With her white lace handkerchief, she gave the lens a gentle clean, then took a photo of the Colossi with the sun blazing on their crumbled faces.

"My goodness," said Jim, arriving at that moment. "Whatever can be going on?"

"See what I mean?" said Pyrella. "Smile, Doris."

Doris obliged, but not too much, otherwise Jim would have to right her beak again, and Pyrella snapped a good shot of her as she sat atop Jim's helmet.

"Why are they all here?" Cairo Jim was amazed. "I know archaeology can be fun at times, but this is quite unexpected."

He brought out his binoculars and peered at the crowd. "How interesting," he said. "Someone has erected a short fence around the base of the statues." He moved his gaze slowly to the left. "Oh, and there's a blackboard with some writing on it."

"What does it say?" asked Doris.

"It's not very neat, and there are one or two spelling mistakes, but it reads: 'Heer Memnon! Next shoe 1 p.m. Admision 50 piastres.'"

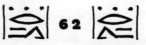

62

"Who's collecting the money?" Pyrella asked. "Surely they'll know what's happening."

Jim surveyed the crowd.

"I can't see anyone selling tickets," he said after a while. "Oh, wait, over near the soft-drink stalls there's an automatic turnstile." He watched intently. "It seems people are putting their money into that and then going into the closest paddock."

He put his binoculars back into Brenda's saddlebag and smiled. "Just think," he said quietly, "after all these years, after all this time, after all the water that's flowed through the Nile, something from the past has returned! I can scarcely believe it's happening. Oh, what a wonderful day this is!"

"Come on," urged Pyrella. "Let's pay up then."

"Too right," said Jim, directing Brenda to the queue.

"Rerk," said Doris, a little bit dubious about the whole thing.

Once they had paid their money, they jostled their way through the crowd until they found a clear patch of ground close to the Colossi.

"How's this?" asked Pyrella.

"Fine," said Jim. "We should be able to hear everything here." His palms were moist with excitement as he unstrapped Brenda's saddle and laid it on the grass. "Now we'll be comfortable. What time is it, Miss Frith?"

Pyrella looked at her watch. "Just after midday," she said.

"Roll on one o'clock," said Jim.

"Hmm," hmmed Doris, scratching at the ground with her claw.

"I've still got time to take a wander and get some shots," Pyrella said. "Will you excuse me, Jim?"

"Of course."

"I'll be back by one." She took her camera and headed off through the noisy crowd.

"Good idea," said Doris. "I might take a little flight myself. To have a look at a few things."

"All right, my dear. See you soon."

"Raark!"

Cairo Jim watched her flutter off over the heads of a nearby family, her beautiful yellow-and-blue plumage bright against the far-off hills. He was about to sit down on the saddle next to Brenda when somebody reached around from behind and tweaked his cheeks.

"Ah, Mr Jim," came a voice. "I knew you would be here."

"Why, Mrs A! Er – it *is* you, isn't it?"

Her hands moved upwards and parted the long bunches of grapes and the dangling bananas which hung from her hat. When her face was visible, Jim saw that it was indeed Mrs Amun-Ra.

"Of course it's me, you silly belly. Did you not know me in my new hat?"

"Not at first," Jim said.

"You like? I bought it with the baksheesh you left the other day."

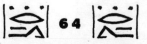

"Yes, it's very – it's very fruity, isn't it?"

"You think I'm the bee's kneecaps then?"

"Er, yes, certainly," stammered Jim, who had not been confronted by so much fruit in a long time. "I like the pineapple on the top especially."

Mrs Amun-Ra touched him lightly on the arm and whispered secretively. "Don't you tell a double soul – it's all made from plastic!"

"Plastic? Really?"

"It must be, you know. Real fruit would not last five minutes in sun such as we have here in Egypt."

"No, I suppose not," said Jim. "It's very sensible when you come to think of it. Would you care to join us, Mrs A? Doris has just flown off for a little while, and Miss Frith is taking some pictures, but they'll be back soon."

"I would delighted be." She put down her carpetbag and sat on the saddle. Jim put his pith helmet back on and sat on the ground between Mrs Amun-Ra and Brenda (who had fallen asleep after the journey).

"Oh," Mrs Amun-Ra sighed, settling herself, "such an important day, is it not?"

"I've waited a long time for something like this," said Jim.

"My, what a lot of people have up turned," she gasped, peering through her grapes. "Anybody who is everybody in Gurna and Luxor are here. Look," she pointed, "there's the Hapi family. They keep the cows, you know. There's Mr Hapi and there's Mrs Hapi. Oh, but I don't much care for the hat *she* is wearing. It makes her look like an ostrich, don't you think so, Mr Jim?"

Jim looked carefully. "In a way, yes, I suppose it does," he answered.

"A woman with a nose like that should not put feathers on her head, I always say. Fruit is much more becoming."

"Are those their children with them?"

Mrs Amun-Ra hoisted some bananas away from her eyes. "Oh, yes," she said. "That is little Cleo and her brother, Travis. He is a very naughty boy, he always has been."

"Why is little Cleo's hair sticking up stiffly like that?"

"Because of Travis. Two weeks ago he put glue in it to make her look like Nefertiti. His mother was most displeased, I can tell you."

"How awful," said Jim.

"It was not as awful as the time he concreted the cat into their front veranda," said Mrs Amun-Ra.

"Why would he do such a thing?"

"He thought their house needed a sphinx to guard it. His mother spanked him till the cows came home. Ah, but they are a happy family, those Hapis, despite Travis's naughty ways. Even the cat has settled down to its new life as a doorstop and paperweight."

She stretched her legs out in front of her and sighed. "So tell me, my friend, are you any closer to the discovery of our Pharaoh yet?"

"Every day we get closer, Mrs A," Jim said. "I think that very soon we'll all be surprised by what turns up."

"Me, I hope so. You are deserving of it greatly. Why, I know of no other archaeologist in the whole of Egypt— Aarrgh! Oh my goodness!" She waved her arms wildly at the pineapple on the top of her hat.

Cairo Jim jumped up to see what all the fuss was about. When he saw the cause of it he said, "It's all right, Mrs A, don't worry."

"But what is it, Mr Jim? All so suddenly I feel this thing on my head as if a little bomb has been dropped there, and much tugging and pulling. What is happening?"

"I think someone else knows better than we do."

"What? I do not understand."

Jim tapped his foot on the ground two or three times. "Doris?" he called.

From around the side of the enormous pineapple Doris poked a wary beak. "Yes?" she said, ruffling her feathers.

"That's Mrs A's hat you're trying to stuff your face with."

She leaned over the brim and stared down at Mrs Amun-Ra. "Salutations."

"Hello, Miss Doris. What are you up to?"

"Sorry, Mrs Amun-Ra, I got hungry. From the air it looked like a feast: Everything so scrumptious, especially the raspberries and these little green things." She hopped down and went to Jim, where she did an embarrassed sort of dance at his feet.

"Oh, you have a stomach like a bottomless pit," laughed Mrs Amun-Ra, patting her hat to make sure her

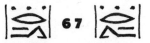

fruit was in place.

"You should be more eagle-eyed next time, Doris," said Jim. He sat down next to her and whispered, "It's all plastic."

"You don't say?" she grimaced. "I don't think my aerial eyesight is what it used to be, somehow. Just before I came here, I saw a rather fetching toucan over on the other side of the paddock. I swooped down and was chatting to him for nearly five minutes before the woman underneath reached up and took him off her head. I *thought* it was a funny place to roost."

She scratched herself and plonked against Jim's leg. "Perhaps I need some new desert sun-spectacles."

"Ah, no," said Mrs Amun-Ra, "what you need is some food. That will buckle up your spirits."

She fossicked around in her carpetbag and brought out a bundle wrapped in one of her tea-shop napkins. "And I have just the very thing," she smiled. "Look, my dears, shergolds for all!"

"Even special snail ones?" asked Doris.

"Even special snail ones, for the likes of you."

"Preerraarrk," preerraarrked Doris happily.

"Hurry up, you acrimonious carrion, we haven't got all day."

Desdemona shot a venomous glare at Bone as he sat on a nearby rock fanning his face with his tangerine fez and smoking a cigar. They had parked the Bugatti at the end of the road so as not to leave tyre tracks and had

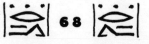

walked for twenty minutes across the rough, dusty ground to Cairo Jim's dig, both of them grumbling about different things all the way.

"I'm working as fast as I can," she hissed. She wedged a stick of dynamite around the other explosives already planted in the hole at the base of the rock pile. "Are you sure this is the right spot?"

"Of course I am."

"The *exact* right spot?"

"I measured it with my archaeological compass and sextant, didn't I? My physics is very good, you know."

"Yes, but—"

"Don't doubt me, Desdemona."

He put his fez back on to protect his balding head from the sun. "Arrr," he breathed, flicking the ash from his cigar into the dust, "I wonder how things are going down near Gurna?" He took his gold fob-watch from his waistcoat pocket and studied it. "We still have half an hour before the greatness commences."

"Plenty of time."

"I hope those Rhampsinites twins get things right."

As she hoisted a tube of gelignite into the hole, Desdemona let out a sinister seaweedy cackle.

"I wish I could see the look on Cairo Jim's face," Bone leered. "Do you know, we're quite lucky in a way."

"Lucky? Rerk! How can we be lucky when one of us has a permanent case of fleas and the other has hopeless delusions of grandeur?"

"I've never had a flea in my life." Bone exhaled his

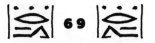

smoke sharply. "You'd get a rock in your gob if you weren't standing so close to those explosives," he seethed. "No, I'll tell you why we're lucky. We're lucky because Cairo Jim is such a dreamer. If he weren't, if he were a more down-to-earth sort of man, I'd have had to come up with something else to get him away from here. Something more believable. But the silly romantic type that he is, he'll fall for the Colossi trick, hook, line and sinker. Arrr. And he's superstitious, too. He still believes in those ancient myths and legends, which will be helpful to us in Part Two of The Plan."

Desdemona hopped up and down on one claw.

"Yes, it's beginning to get exciting, isn't it?" said Bone.

"Exciting, my beak! I've got a flea in a troublesome spot, That's all."

"Get on with the job, you scrofulous thing."

"At least I don't look like I've been inflated with a bicycle pump," she muttered.

"What was that?"

"Nothing, my Captain."

"Hmmph."

Grabbing his telescope, Bone pointed it in the direction of Cairo Jim's camp. His line of vision moved slowly over Jim's carefully patched and mended tent, past Doris's perch (a gift to her from the last Sultan of Zanzibar), past Brenda's camel-post and Jim's shaving-stand and mirror, until it came to the small table where Jim wrote his journal and the occasional poem. There,

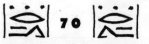

surrounded by fountain pens, coloured pencils, blotting paper, sharpeners and erasers, stood a silver-framed photograph of a woman leaning against the wing of an aeroplane.

Captain Neptune Bone held the telescope very still and squinted hard.

It was Jocelyn Osgood.

He lowered the telescope to his side and bit deeply into his cigar. "Aaaaaarrrrr," he said in a low moan. Desdemona had never before heard him say "Aaaaaarrrrr" like that. She stopped stashing the T.N.T. and stared curiously. There was a peculiar glaze over his eyes, as though someone had just shown him a new colour he had never seen before, or had never even dreamt of. This was most unlike Neptune Bone, she thought.

"Is anything wrong, Captain?" she asked.

But he didn't hear her croaking. He was back in time. Back to the days when he and Jim were still mates, working on the excavation of the Bent Pyramid near Saqqara. A time before either of them had met their feathered companions. All sorts of memories rushed into his mind, like hazy ghosts from a former life. He remembered the day when Jocelyn Osgood had flown into their camp. She had answered an advertisement Cairo Jim had put in the newspaper for someone to help with the dig, and it was the first time either of the archaeologists had met her.

For a month she had worked with them, patiently

blowing the sand away from their hieroglyphs with her small dusting brush. During this time, Bone had observed how she and Jim had got on so well. Famously, in fact, and it had irked him terribly. Whenever he attempted to be pleasant to her, things always went wrong, until he became extremely jealous of the archaeologist-poet. Whenever he saw Jocelyn Osgood sharing a joke with Jim, and heard her bright, infectious laughter filling the camp, he became furious and agitated. Finally, he could take no more. He packed up his belongings and left the excavation, vowing never to return.

It was at this time he decided that human beings (those who were still alive) were a waste of time. In the future, he would pursue three things only: fame, fortune and food.

Now, as he stared out into space, the mere idea of Jocelyn Osgood made parts of him go quite wobbly.

"I said, is anything wrong?"

Bone jerked his head sideways, as if someone had fired a pistol right next to his eardrum. "Mmm?" he murmured.

"You were a million miles away."

"Yes. No. Not a million…"

He puffed his cigar long and deeply. "Tell me something, evil eyes—"

"What is it now?" asked Desdemona as she fetched more gelignite from the bag.

"Tell me this: what does Jocelyn Osgood see in Cairo

Jim? Why does she spend so much time with him?"

Desdemona picked out a spool of fuse-rope from her bag and started to connect it to the sticks and tubes. "It's because he can do poems," she muttered.

"Poems? Because he can do poems? Harrrr!"

"She likes the finer things in an archaeologist."

Bone flung his cigar to the ground and stamped it out grumpily. "Anyone can do poems," he rumbled.

"You can't."

"I can too."

"Betcha can't."

"I bet you I can, clever beak."

She stopped stringing her explosives together and peered schemingly at him. "What do you bet?"

"Anything you want."

"Anything?" Her eyes throbbed redly.

"Anything," said Bone.

"All right. I have one great desire—"

"Name it."

"Before Jim and that gaudy Doris leave the Valley, I want to pluck her."

"You want *what*?"

"I want every single feather from her body. I want to pull them out, one by one, and I want to hear her scream as I do it."

"You really are an evil creature," Bone said, a hint of admiration in his voice. "Whatever will you do with them?"

"I'll make the most beautiful cloak. To wear on

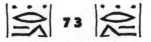 73

special occasions. Black has never suited me, it clashes with my eyes." She pecked a flea from underneath her wing.

"All right, you're on."

"So, do a poem."

"What, right now?"

"Right now."

He rubbed his moustache with the back of his hand several times as he tried to think. "Let me see … what should it be about? Something important, I think, something great. Something dear to my heart. Ah! I know just the thing!"

He crossed his legs and clasped the top of his kneecap.

"Come on then, genius," said Desdemona.

He cleared his throat and began to declaim, pronouncing each word clearly:

My name is Bone,
I'll have it known,
it will be writ and spoke.
I am the best
archaeologest,
the very greatest bloke.

He folded his arms and smirked. "There, gormless, I told you I could do it."

"Bleccchhh," spat Desdemona. "That was dreadful."

"Truth is never dreadful, beetroot brain."

"It didn't even rhyme properly."

"Yes it did."

"My tailfeathers it did. 'Best' and 'archaeologest' don't rhyme."

Bone scowled for a moment. "When you are carried away by the passion of your art they do," he said smugly. "But of course you wouldn't understand that, would you, cantankerous claws? The only thing you feel passionate about is seaweed."

"And the feathers of Doris, don't forget them."

"Oh, yes, them too."

"So I can have them?"

"You haven't won our bet—"

"That was no poem."

"—but because I'm such a generous man, I'll grant your wish."

"Oh, you're too kind," she said sarcastically.

"Yes, lesser men admire me for it."

He examined his fob-watch again and became business-like. "We must get a move on, bird. Soon the event will be starting."

"Almost there, almost, almost, almost…"

Bone snapped the watch-cover shut. "When you've done all the fusing, you must dig a shallow trench from the rock pile to Cairo Jim's tent, and then lay the wire into it."

"And then?"

"Then bury it carefully, all the way along the trench, and make sure you brush away all claw prints. You must leave the end of the fuse poking above the ground, but cover it with a rock, otherwise that meddlesome camel might find it."

Desdemona stopped connecting the explosives and looked through her slitted, throbbing eyes at him. "And you?" she asked. "What are you going to do?"

"First of all, I'll take a stroll down to the dig. There I'll drop this lifelike lithograph of Rin Tin Tin in a noticeable spot." He stood and withdrew the lithograph from the back pocket of his plus-fours. "When I return, I'll rid the air of your stinky presence and we can be off."

"Don't strain yourself, will you?" She pecked a small hole into the final stick of dynamite and inserted the end of the fuse. Then she started to tie all the ropes together to form one lethal chain.

"A genius never does," said Bone, heading down the hill towards the dig.

"Ah, Miss Pyrella, come and join us before this greedy bird scoffs all the shergolds!"

"Hello, Mrs Amun-Ra," said Pyrella, finishing off her vanilla ice-cream. "My, that's quite a load of fruit up there."

"The fruit of life," Mrs Amun-Ra said, "is best eaten fresh, you know."

"That's very good, Mrs A," said Jim. "Who said that?"

"I did, just now. I made it up."

"Ah." He turned to Pyrella. "Get any good shots?"

"I don't think so. Too many people in the way."

She removed her gloves, then took a bottle of sunscreen lotion from the pocket of her skirt and squeezed the white fluid into the palm of her hand. "I do wish it weren't quite so hot," she said, rubbing the lotion vigorously onto her arms. Then she found her roll-on insect repellent and proceeded to apply it slowly all over her exposed areas.

"Never mind," Jim said, "soon you won't even notice the heat. I was just telling Mrs A and Doris how Alexander the Great once brought his entire court here many centuries ago. They picnicked on this very spot while they waited for the Colossi to blast their trumpets."

"How exciting," said Mrs Amun-Ra. "To think I am sitting where Alexander's Greatness once was." She shifted on the saddle.

Brenda snored loudly.

Pyrella put away the insect repellent and looked at her watch. "One o'clock exactly," she announced.

"The hour has arrived," breathed Jim, fidgeting with his sun-spectacles.

"*Prark!*" Doris took a last chomp on her shergold and jumped up onto Jim's shoulder. He stood to get a better view.

Suddenly there was a loud, crackling hiss and the crowd fell silent. People stopped eating their sandwiches and guzzling their soft drinks. Babies ceased crying and gurgling, camels stood about chewing silently, donkeys brayed no more. Travis Hapi forgot about catching flies to put into his sister's stiff hair and looked towards the Colossi, biting his lip. Even Brenda the Wonder Camel woke up, knowing that the time had come.

But no one in the whole gathering awaited the miracle more eagerly than Cairo Jim.

Then there was a noisy blowing, followed by three dull tapping noises, and an electrical screech, high pitched and awful. Many people shuddered and put their hands over their ears.

When the screeching finally died away, a voice crackled: "Testing, one, two—"

There was a pause. Pyrella looked quizzically at Jim.

"Three," said another, fainter voice.

"Three," crackled the first voice. "It's working."

"Get on with it," urged the faint voice.

The crackling voice cleared its throat. "Good afternoon, ladies and gentlemen and everyone else. Welcome to the most amazing thing to happen in Egypt in a long long time. We hope you enjoy the show, but we must remind you that the taking of photographs or the recording of the performance is strictly pro–pro—"

"Prohibited," hissed the faint voice.

"Prohibited."

"Those voices sound familiar," Doris whispered in Jim's ear.

"Yes," he frowned, "they do, don't they?"

"And now, without any further ado, let us present to you, for the first time in hundreds of years, the fantastic

Colossi of Lemons!"

There was a thumping noise, followed by a loud "Yowwww!"

"Memnon," the faint voice said. "The fantastic Colossi of Memnon."

"The fantastic Colossals of Memnon."

"Blunderer! Give me that." The faint voice became louder. "And one last thing, ladies and gentlemen and everyone else. If you would like to buy a souvenir of this glorious occasion, they will be on sale near the entrance turnstile at the end of the performance. And now, the Colossi!"

"Right," said Jim, "That's it. I think we should get to the bottom of this, Doris."

He reached down and yanked his umbrella from out of Brenda's saddlebag.

"Excuse me, Mrs A."

"Oh, Mr Jim," squirmed Mrs Amun-Ra.

"But Jim, aren't you going to stay and listen?"

"I'll hear everything from its source, Miss Frith."

Brenda snorted and stomped.

"No, Brenda, you stay here and keep an eye on things. We won't be long."

Doris and Jim headed off through the expectant crowd, excusing themselves as they brushed through the huddled groups.

When they were almost at the fence at the base of the Colossi, trumpet music started to play.

The tune was not at all what Pyrella Frith had

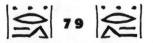

expected. Sitting on the grass where Jim and Doris had left them, she turned to Mrs Amun-Ra. "How odd," she said.

"I know that song, Miss Pyrella. It I have heard on the wireless sometimes. What is it called ... 'The Picnic of the Teddy Bears'?"

Pyrella nodded. "'The Teddy Bears' Picnic.' A strange song for Colossi such as these. Still, I suppose even they have to move with the times."

"I suppose so too," said Mrs Amun-Ra, tapping her feet happily to the rhythm.

Jim and Doris jumped the fence and darted quickly to one of the statues. There, they ducked close to the crumbling stone and began to edge their way around to the rear.

"Stay close, Doris," Jim whispered.

She crouched under the brim of his pith helmet and nestled in close to his neck, while he grasped his umbrella as though it were a rapier.

"Get ready, get set, *go!*"

Together they leapt around the corner, Jim thrusting the umbrella into the air.

They stood still for a moment, surprised at the empty space. Then Doris noticed something.

"Over there, Jim, behind the other statue. Look."

There they saw the Rhampsinites twins squatting on the ground, both of them hunched over a wind-up antique gramophone connected to a large amplifier and speakers. They were nodding their bristly heads in time

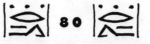

to the music and grinning. Behind them, their wheel-barrow was overflowing with scarabs, and a rusty microphone lay discarded on the ground.

"I might have known," said Cairo Jim.

He and Doris crept up stealthily, until they were a few paces behind them.

"The game's up, you rotten swizzlers!" shouted Jim.

Abdullah Rhampsinites turned quickly. "It's Cairo Jim," he gasped, his eye wide with terror. "We've been found out!"

"You certainly have, Kelvin."

"Abdullah."

"You certainly have, Abdullah. What's the meaning of this—this poppycock?" Jim's blood started to boil.

"We'd better scram, brother," squealed Abdullah.

"Oh, just when things were going so well, too," whined Kelvin. He sprang up and made a dash for the wheelbarrow, but Jim and Doris were too quick for him. They jumped in front of it, Jim's umbrella at the ready, and barred Kelvin's way.

"Not so fast, you blackguard," threatened Jim.

Abdullah flipped the gramophone needle off the record and disconnected it from the amplifier. Then, tucking the machine under his skinny arm, he started to scramble in the opposite direction.

"After him, Doris," commanded Jim.

"*Raaaaaaaaaarrrrrkkk!*"

After him she flew, her wings menacing about his head, as he fled to the hills behind the Colossi.

"Please, Cairo Jim," pleaded Kelvin, "Show mercy. I was only doing what I was told."

"Mercy? I'll show you mercy, you scoundrel." In a rare moment of anger, he threw down his umbrella and grabbed Kelvin Rhampsinites by the shoulders. Turning him around, Jim gave his uttermost portions a thwacking kick. It was so hard and sudden it propelled Kelvin out of his green sandals and into the air.

"*Yooooooowwwwwwww*," he screamed. He landed on the ground with a huge thud.

"Don't you ever show your face around here again," yelled Jim.

Kelvin picked himself up and, rubbing his bruises, took off quickly, tripping up in his galabiyya as he stumbled after his terrified brother.

In the paddock, the people were milling about, wondering why the music had come to such an abrupt end.

Presently they found out.

"Testing, testing. Ladies and gentlemen and everyone else, this is Cairo Jim speaking. You may be wondering why the show has stopped so suddenly. Well, it is my melancholy duty to tell you that we have all been tricked."

There were gasps of disbelief from the crowd.

"These mighty Colossi did not play for you today. What you heard was in fact part of an underhand scheme perpetrated by those tasteless, rude brothers, the Rhampsinites twins. They have attempted to present this

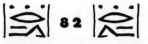 82

hoax for reasons of greed – to make money for themselves by swindling you. But rest assured, they have not been successful. With the help of my colleague Doris, they have been booted out and are now, at this very moment, fleeing to the hills. Ladies and gentlemen and everyone else, I will personally smash open the turnstile and return every piastre of your admission money. And, courtesy of those impudent, contemptuous felons, there will be free plastic scarabs for every child in the audience."

A half-hearted "hooray" went up from some parts of the crowd.

Then Mrs Amun-Ra shouted, "Three cheers for Mr Cairo Jim and Miss Doris," and the crowd obliged enthusiastically, some men even throwing their fezzes into the air.

Doris flew back and perched on the handle of the wheelbarrow as Jim turned off the microphone.

"I let him go," she said. "But not until he got a good dose of my feathers."

"Good work, my dear," said Jim sadly. He picked up his umbrella and drew circles in the dirt. "What a crashing disappointment this has turned out to be."

"Never mind, Jim. There are more important things in heaven and earth…"

He looked at her, a glimmer of a smile starting to appear on his face.

"Shakespeare," she prowked. "Well, almost…"

"You're right, my friend. There *are* more important things. And we must go and dig for one of them, just as

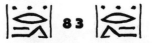

83

soon as I've fixed up all this money business."

"Rark. That's more like it. Come on then."

"Too right," said Cairo Jim, extending his arm. The noble macaw came and took her place, and together they went to face the crowd.

Five minutes later, Miss Pyrella Frith watched as Jim and Doris began to refund the admission money to the long queue of spectators. "Poor Jim," she said quietly.

"Ah, those rotten Rhampsinites twins," said Mrs Amun-Ra, tidying up her shergold napkins and patting down her cherries. "Wait until their mother hears about this. Why, from now on I would not give them the time of night, not even if they asked for it. Scallywigs!"

"—and Captain Bone, that is not all. My poor brother has a large bruise in the shape of Cairo Jim's boot all over his backside."

"You don't say?"

"Perhaps you would like to see it? Brother, come here—"

"No, no, no, I'll take your word for it."

"It's very nasty."

"I'm sure. Where's my gramophone?"

Abdullah lifted his galabiyya and stepped aside. There on the ground lay a pile of wood and machinery.

"I'm afraid I dropped it when the bird known as Doris was chasing me," he said.

Bone was aghast. "Heavens to Betsy," he gasped.

"Leave Auntie out of this," Kelvin said.

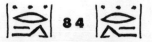

"Do you have any idea how much that cost? That was a very valuable piece."

"So is my brother's backside," said Abdullah. "He is now finding it quite difficult to sit down properly. He falls off chairs, if you want to know. I think you should pay us a little extra for his discomfort."

Bone got up from his deep armchair and puffed smoke into Abdullah's face. "Now, listen to me, Kelvin—"

"I am Abdullah."

"I don't care who you are, you toothless moron, listen. By my reckoning, you have only just carried out my orders. It was because of sheer fortune, and not your efforts, that the hoax went on for as long as it did. But seeing as how I'm such a magnanimous chap, I will pay you what we agreed. The loss of the gramophone, however, will have to come out of your fee."

"Oh, please, Captain Bone, be reasonable."

"I'm being more than reasonable, you savagely haircutted man. Now, we agreed on five pounds, I think."

"No, Captain, it was ten."

"Five."

"Ten," insisted Abdullah.

Bone fixed him with an evil stare. "Desdemona has a good memory for numbers. Would you like me to call her?"

Abdullah froze. That was the last thing he wanted. "I remember now, it *was* five," he said hurriedly.

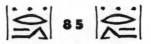

"Right," said Bone. "Now, I estimate the cost of repairs to my gramophone will be at least fifteen pounds. So that's ten pounds you owe me."

"How do you think my brother and I can come up with that kind of money?" laughed Abdullah scornfully. "We are trying to save to buy our mother—"

"Are you saying you don't have it?"

"No, we don't," said Kelvin, rubbing his backside.

Bone sighed and cracked his knuckles loudly. "All right. In that case, you both owe me a favour."

"A favour? What do you mean?"

"I'll think of something, don't either of you worry."

"But Captain Bone—"

"I've had enough of you now. Be off with you both." He turned on his heel.

"But I implore you," began Abdullah.

"Desdemona!" called Bone.

The raven poked her beak, stuffed into a tin of seaweed, around the door-flap of Bone's tent-pavilion. She was cranky at being disturbed and her eyes throbbed angrily.

"Oh, no, not her. We go, we go right now. Come, Abdullah."

"But I am Kelvin," Kelvin said.

Abdullah looked at his brother, then carefully at himself. Then he walloped Kelvin on the arm. "Come on anyway, you blunderer!" he hissed.

"Ouch! Bully-boy."

And off they skulked.

Desdemona regarded Bone, who was studying the mess which had up until recently been his beloved gramophone. She slunk her head back into the tent-pavilion and continued to enjoy her tinned feast.

"If you want anything done properly, you have to do it yourself," snarled the fleshy man as he nudged the pieces with his shoe and began to contemplate the next part of The Plan.

A QUIET MOMENT

THAT NIGHT, underneath a glowing sky, Cairo Jim wrote a postcard to Jocelyn Osgood.

Dear Jocelyn Osgood,

Many peculiar things have taken place here lately. Doris, Brenda & I left the dig today to go to hear the Colossi play their tune. But it turned out to be the most terrible hoax, organised by two money-grubbing brothers who are well known in these parts for their greed & tastelessness. What a fizzer, I can tell you.

Our search for Martenarten continues. We have been spurred on by the discovery of a small brooch which dates from the King's reign, & every day I feel sure we are getting closer.

Also, we keep finding the most unexpected series of pictures in our dig, all of famous people or animals. The latest (I found it tonight) is of Rin Tin Tin. It's all very strange & we don't know what to make of it.

Well, Jocelyn Osgood, even though I have written as small as I can, I am running out of room now. I will tell you much more when I see

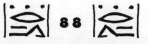

you, which I hope will be soon. We are all well &
roaring, hope you are likewise.

Your good friend,

C. Jim.

P.S. When you visit again, could you pls bring
some more ribbons for Doris? She doesn't say as
much, but I know she would love some new ones.

Somewhere in the hills, a jackal howled at the moon.
Jim read through what he had written, then took some
blotting paper and blotted the postcard carefully.

Doris sat on her perch, fast asleep. They had worked
hard at the dig after returning from the Colossi and she
was now thoroughly exhausted. Her belly was full with
snails and the feathers on her chest ruffled gently
whenever she exhaled.

Brenda the Wonder Camel was sitting on the floor in
Jim's tent, her rear legs crossed comfortably as she
engrossed herself in a new book. It was one of her
favourite kinds, a Western adventure story, complete
with illustrations. She was enjoying it very much and
wishing she were the cowboy's best horse.

Jim turned up the kerosene lamp and gazed at his
photograph of Jocelyn Osgood. As he lost himself in
her wide smile, a soft rhythm started to come to him,
over and over, on and on, until it was firmly set in his
mind. Then words began to follow the rhythm, the
sorts of words he always remembered whenever he

thought of her. Some of them joined themselves together to form rhymes, and before he knew it, Cairo Jim had a poem.

He pulled out a piece of clean writing paper from the back of his journal and quickly began to write it down:

Oh Jocelyn, Jocelyn Osgood,
you Valkyrie of the Skies,
you are the best Chief Stewardess
of anyone who flies.

Your auburn hair, pulled back so tight,
your neatly pleated skirt,
your silver torch's moonbeam light,
those shoes that never hurt.

Your pearly teeth, your winged lapel,
that uniform of grey,
your perfume with the rosy smell,
the horns on your beret.

Those breastplates you wear on your chest,
your reassuring manner,
the way you wear your sweet life-vest,
your aircraft wrench and spanner.

Oh Jocelyn, Jocelyn Osgood,
you are so far away,
while we're digging for a mighty King

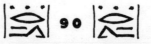

from a long-lost yesterday…

But Jocelyn, Jocelyn Osgood,
away in Casablanca,
there is one thing my heart does sing –
it is for you I hanker.

He sucked the lid of his fountain pen for several
moments, not quite sure about "Casablanca" and the
last word. Then he smiled, blotted the poem, and tucked
it into the secret pouch in the inside back cover of his
journal.

After all, there are some things that not even Doris
should know.

MORE SKULDUGGERY
AND DESPAIR

TWILIGHT SAT TREMBLING on the horizon.

The day's heat rose from the earth, making the air shimmer in the fading light. The approaching night had not brought its coolness yet; it was still very hot, and Cairo Jim's skin prickled as he lay on his rickety camp bed, staring at the moon through an unpatched hole in the roof of his tent.

"That planet," he reflected, "is the same now as it was in ancient times. The same shape, the same height, the same colours."

He closed his eyes and thought of the ways the moon had been seen by humans through time. Musicians had written songs about it, painters had put it in their paintings and, by the light of its silvery beams, people had fallen in love. Why, humans had even landed on it. And some had even *danced* on it.

Jim suddenly opened his eyes, his train of thought stopped abruptly by the image of Buzz Aldrin dancing in his huge white spacesuit. He lit his lamp and directed the light onto the wall of the tent. The gallery of pictures that had puzzled him for so long hung there, staring down at him, almost taunting him.

"Right," he said aloud. "I'm going to sort this thing out." He reached under his pillow and took out a small notepad (which he kept there in case a poem came to him in the middle of the night) and pencil. Then he called for Doris.

She blew into the dusky tent and nestled at the end of the bed. "Rerk. I'm glad you called. I've been trying to get Brenda interested in a game of pontoon, but she's got her head buried in some old cowboy story. When that camel starts on a book, nothing can distract her..."

"My dear, I want to work all these out." He gestured to the pinned-up pictures. "I want you to help me."

"Work them out? What do you mean?"

Jim chewed the end of the pencil before he spoke. "Well, it seems to me there's something behind it. It can't be a mere coincidence that six pictures have turned up for no explicable reason, can it? I mean, when we found Buzz Aldrin, I didn't think much of it. But then Edith Sitwell followed and I started to take a bit of notice. Then William the Conqueror arrived and really got my mind ticking. Alice B. Toklas bamboozled me, Rin Tin Tin further complicated the conundrum, until this afternoon when Ethelred the Unready hit me on the head and made me realise that it may be some sort of message."

Doris stretched her wings. "Message?" she asked. "From whom?"

He stared at the pictures, his eyes trying to pierce them for a clue. "That's not the question. What we need

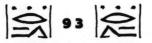

to know is, *what does it all mean?*"

"Let's get to work then," she flarped.

Which is exactly what they did.

Firstly, they tried to work out if there was any link between the subjects. They determined that:

1. Buzz Aldrin was an astronaut with an unusual first name

2. Edith Sitwell was a poet with an unusual last name

3. William the Conqueror was a king with a horse

4. Alice B. Toklas was a writer with an unusual middle name (or so thought Doris until Jim pointed out that the "B" was in fact short for something, but when Doris asked him what, he had to admit he didn't know)

5. Rin Tin Tin was a dog who had spent most of his time barking a lot and rescuing children from swollen rivers, and

6. Ethelred the Unready was a king with an equally unusual first and last name.

They both agreed that that exercise didn't help them much at all.

Jim decided on a new approach. Maybe, he said, there was some sort of code contained in the letters of their names. Being good at hieroglyphs, Doris volunteered to try to crack it if there was one, so Jim wrote down: BUZZALDRINEDITHSITWELLWILLIAMTHECONQUERORALIC EBTOKLASRINTINTINETHELREDTHEUNREADY.

Doris began an intense scrutiny. Every so often she

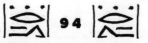

made a small crooning noise, then a tch-tch sound, and then she would scratch her plumage. Sometimes she thought she had it, but at the last moment she would find that there were insufficient letters, and it would all fall to pieces. For example, she could make:

"On Wednesday I like to swim in the Nile and tether Brenda to the bullchair till I quit. Rearrc. Uzzll."

Or, "Come in to the casbah and all nuzzle quietly under the brilliant red kettle while I sit down. Riirr."

But they were not very useful.

She continued unscrambling for some time, until she ended up with: "Be kind and direct me at the nearest ocelot, Raquel, I need to buy it a thin williswirzzlir. Hurhnlll."

At this point, Jim decided they were getting nowhere fast.

Outside, all was quiet, deathly quiet, the only noises being the sound of Brenda turning the pages of her novel and the occasional appreciative snort.

"Let's try something simpler," Jim said. He tore off the sheet of paper and crumpled it into a ball. On the next page he wrote BAESWTCABTRTTETU.

"Five vowels, eleven consonants," said Doris. "Let's see…" She made a series of small clucking sounds while she thought. "How about this? Trace base tub—no, that's no good, there's still a 'w' and three 't's left. Hmm. What about tube bat tatters wc?"

"I don't think so," frowned Jim.

"I know, I know, I've got it!" She hopped up and

down on Jim's blanket. "Swat bet butter cat."

"Swat bet butter cat?"

"It uses up all the letters," she said hopefully.

Jim wrote down the words and looked at them. "Swat bet butter cat," he read. "Swat cat butter bet? Cat butter bet swat? Butter cat swat bet? No," he said, scribbling them out. "I think we're still barking up the wrong tree. Let's see what happens with this," and he quickly jotted ASCTTU.

Doris looked at him, wondering.

"The first letter of each last name," he told her.

She studied them for a minute, then said, "No. No good at all."

He crossed out those and, with a sigh, wrote down six more letters.

When he and Doris saw what appeared on the page before them, their blood froze.

All at once, a strong breeze swept into the tent. The hot wind carried an awful smell, a stale aroma of ancient graves laced with musty cigar smoke. Jim covered his mouth with his handkerchief to avoid the stench. The pictures moved back and forth unsteadily against the billowing canvas, and the pages of his notepad were ripped off one by one and flung against the rear wall of the tent by the rising wind.

"Raaaark!" cried Doris, trying to keep her balance on the end of the bed.

The lamp slid along the bedside table and would have crashed to the ground, had Jim not lunged to grab it.

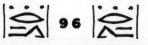

Then, as quickly as it had come, the turbulence died down to a faint, humid whisper, and they heard a voice in the falling darkness.

"Cairo Jim," it came. "Cairo Jim. Cairo Jiiiiiiiiiim."

Jim and Doris stayed where they were and peered out through the door.

"Listen," said Doris, her feathers standing on end. "What's that?"

A dull dragging noise could be heard, as though something heavy were being pulled through the dust. It seemed to be coming closer.

By the flickering lamplight, a large, bandaged figure lurched into view. The being was tatty, yellow and towering. Its arms were crossed over its chest, the bandages over its eyes blackened by the soot of ages, and the top of its head was defined by a squat cylindrical shape under the wraps. There was a tiny hole where its mouth was. Out of this came muffled wheezes.

Both Jim's and Doris's breathing almost stopped as they stared at the visitor.

"Who–who are you and what do you want?" Jim managed to ask.

The creature raised its right arm and turned the palm of its bandaged hand to them. It spoke with a low rumble, its voice like thunder from a far-away mountain peak.

"I am Mar–ten–art–en," it said. "Pharaoh of Egypt, King of all the land and its people, Servant and Messenger of Ta, the Great God and Keeper of the Moon."

The breeze puffed up again, blowing through the bandages and into the tent.

"I am here in *anger*..."

Cairo Jim's stomach clenched under the withering, black-as-nothing gaze.

"Be warned, Cairo Jim. Whomsoever attempts to disturb my final resting place will have the Curses of the Pharaohs haunt them for the rest of their life, and their children's, and their dogs'. Take *heed* of this warning. You have angered the Great Ta, who even now looks upon you, *frowning*. He has sent many messages to you in his own mysterious way," and here, the creature turned its outstretched hand towards the wall of pictures, "but you have chosen to ignore the signs. You must *not* continue to search for my Tomb. You must *leave* this place, taking everything with you, and you must *never* return."

The thing began to back slowly away from them.

"Go from this place," it continued, its spectral voice rising more and more. "Incur the wrath of Ta no longer. *Go, and leave me for evermore* – leave me to rest for all eternity!"

There followed a single second of absolute silence.

Then suddenly the air was rocketed by a terrific, almost deafening explosion. It was the most monstrous noise ever heard in ancient or modern Egypt.

Booooooooooooooooooooooooooooooooooooooooooooooooooooooom!

A gigantic mushroom cloud of smoke rose up and up, higher and higher, spreading out to the stars.

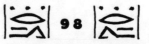

The force of the blast ripped the tent from its pegs and hurled it into the sky. It went soaring, the canvas beating wildly, with all its contents, including Jim and Doris, tumbling from one end to the other.

It came to land in a heap several metres from where it had been pitched. Unhurt except for a few bruises, Jim and Doris crawled out from under the canvas heap to find their camp smothered in a fog of rising dust. Pieces of rock and grit fell from the air, narrowly missing them.

The mummy of Pharaoh Martenarten was nowhere to be seen, having vanished into the thick dust cover.

"Quaaaaoooo," came a snorting cough.

"Brenda!" screeched Doris.

Jim ran to the Wonder Camel and found her clutching the cover of her book, her hoofs trembling. All of the pages inside had been blown clear away and this upset her as much as the explosion, for she had been in the middle of the final chapter, and the action had been hotting up considerably.

"Brenda! My lovely, are you all right?"

She gave herself a quick looking-over, then nodded her head.

"We're all okay then. That's the main thing."

Doris squawked loudly. "Jim, the rock pile…"

He looked towards the patch of completely levelled ground where the tonnes of debris had been. "For the love of Rameses," he gasped.

"But where's it gone?" Doris flapped.

"Quick!" Jim shouted. "To the dig!"

They snatched a lantern on the way and raced as fast as they could, all three of them skidding down the rocky slope near the entrance of the dig.

The scene resembled a battlefield. All of their work was now buried once again.

The situation was hopeless. Stones, rocks and rubble had avalanched all the way to the opening of the tunnel, sealing it absolutely.

"Months," said Jim in a strangled voice, for he was hardly able to speak. "Everything. Gone." In disbelief, he kicked a rock into the mess. "All gone."

Doris watched him as he pottered around the carnage, his shoulders stooped in a way she had never seen. She tried to think of something to say, but no quotes from Shakespeare sprang to her mind. The chain of events was too bewildering, too horrendous, and she knew that not even the immortal Bard could lighten the awful despair which had exploded into their world. So she remained silent and very, very sad.

Brenda, too, was heartbroken. For the first time in her Bactrian life, she felt quite Wonderless.

As Cairo Jim poked about in the dreadful mess, he felt as though some giant's hand had pulled his soul out through his ribcage and had flung it into the dust, where it would swirl about in the wind until it was dissolved by time into a billion specks of nothing.

He was utterly empty.

Minutes passed. Dumbfounded minutes, hazy

minutes, minutes crammed with confusion and bewilderment, until Jim could not stay there any longer.

"Come on, gang," he said to his friends without looking at them. "We have a camp to re-erect." But he knew in his heart it might not be for long.

The animals followed him up the slope of rubble and slowly, their feet as heavy as concrete blocks, they trudged back to the campsite.

Over the hills, in the Valley of the Queens, Desdemona dreamed of the beautiful cloak which would soon be hers. She sniggered out of the side of her beak as she unwrapped Bone from his bandages.

"Arrr," he winced, "these bandages stink. Couldn't you have pinched some newer ones?"

"Moan, moan, moan," said the raven. "You're never satisfied."

"Phah! They reek of the grave!"

"What do you expect? I pulled them out of a tomb display in the Luxor Museum when the guard wasn't looking."

He flicked her on the top of her skull.

"Erk! What was that for?"

"I felt like it. I have to admit it, bird, you did surprisingly well this evening."

"You are too kind," she muttered.

"Yes. You *did* deliver the brass rubbing of Ethelred the Unready to the dig, didn't you?"

"This afternoon. When I flew over and unburied the

fuse wire. You were waxing your moustache at the time. I dropped it right on Cairo Jim's pith helmet."

"What? He didn't see you, did he?"

"Not likely. I scarpered as quick as I could."

"Good."

"Now for your legs. Be swashbuckling," she told him, then added under her breath, "for once in your life."

Bone parted his legs and she started unwrapping one of them.

"I don't know why you didn't get one of those Rhampsinites twins to dress up. It would've saved a lot of work. They owe you a favour."

"Not after yesterday's fiasco with my gramophone. Anyway, I wanted this pleasure all for myself. The Scaring of Cairo Jim was my special dessert, if you get my meaning. The superstitious excavationist was so terrified, he jumped clear out of his sock-garters. Arrr. And then, when everything went boom, it really put the wind up his obelisks."

Desdemona cackled. "I hope Doris's snazzy beak dropped off!" She stopped unbandaging and pecked Bone on the knee. "Remember, I want those feathers," she crowed.

"Ouch! I promised you, didn't I? Before they scram, you can have them." He flexed his calf muscles impatiently and inspected his hands. "Blast," he muttered, "two fingernails chipped. And I'd only just manicured."

"Was I right on cue when I lit the fuse?" asked the

throbbing one.

"Mm? Oh, yes, I couldn't have done it better myself. 'Eternity'. Right on cue."

"Eternity," she echoed, cackling all the more raucously. "Nevermore, nevermore, nevermore. Ha ha ha ha ha ha ha!"

Her laughter was infectious. Neptune Bone eyed the silver-framed photograph of Jocelyn Osgood which he had swiped from Jim's table as he had made his mummified exit. Then he threw back his head and bellowed thunderously into the shattered night.

The tent was finally up again. Doris and Brenda knew that this was one of those times when Jim needed to be alone with his thoughts, so they bade him goodnight and went outside, Doris to her Zanzibar perch and the Wonder Camel to try to find a patch of comfortable ground which had not been ripped apart by the explosion.

As Jim sat heavily on his bed, he spied one of the sheets of notepad paper scrunched between the end of the bed and the rear wall of the tent. He reached down and picked it up.

Underneath the scribbled-out letters and words, he read the final thing he had written before the visitation. Six single letters. BEWARE. Once again, his blood chilled.

He screwed the paper into a tight ball and threw it to the floor. Reaching out, he turned down the lamp until the flame flickered away to nothing. Then, still fully clothed, he lay his head on the hard, flat pillow, knowing that tonight he would not sleep at all.

In the cool, potted-palmed, marble-floored, cedar-panelled clubroom of the Old Relics Society in Cairo, two gentlemen sat in sumptuous leather armchairs, each grimly sipping a Belzoni Whopper.*

The elder of the two had sad eyes and a thin, sunken face half covered by a neatly trimmed pair of muttonchop sideburns which joined his grey moustache. His name was Esmond Horneplush, and he had been a member of the Society for more than forty years. For many of those years he had worked as an archaeologist out in the field, but he had never made any discoveries of especially startling merit, and now he was content to sit in the clubroom with his friends and colleagues, reminiscing about the good old days and occasionally imagining, with wetted lips and sparkling eyes, what might have been.

His companion on this particular afternoon was a possum-faced gentleman with short dark hair and an upturned moustache. Around the corners of his small eyes lay an intricate network of criss-crossed wrinkles, the result of spending too much time in the sun without

---

*A fruity drink named after Giovanni Battista Belzoni, the ex-circus strongman who in 1818 became the first European to enter the pyramid of Chephren.

 104

wearing proper desert sun-spectacles. His cheeks were rounded and pink and his baggy white linen suit had seen more prosperous days. He was Gerald Perry Esquire, and he was busy lamenting his latest business venture.

"Thought it'd be a smash," he muttered, playing with one of the tiny paper umbrellas in his Belzoni Whopper. "No one'd ever done pigeons before, not on this scale. Do you know the sorts of things I had planned, Horneplush?"

"Hmm? No, I can't say I do," answered Esmond Horneplush, who was studying a spidery crack in the opposite wall and trying to calculate how many years it would take before it reached the doorframe.

"Let me tell you. Pigeon burgers, pigeon rissoles, fillets of pigeon, pigeon nuggets with three special sauces, special boxes of pigeon wings, pigeon and galletas saladas – that's Spanish for 'salted crackers', did you know?"

"Mm? No, Spanish is not a language I—"

"Pigeon and crackers, fried pigeon, baked pigeon, steamed, grilled and braised pigeon, pigeon Wellington, pigeon con habas (that's with beans), filet pigeon, pigeon and spaghetti. All in neat takeaway cartons. Convenient and clean. Guaranteed no mess. And everything served promptly, with a cheery smile, by one of our helpful staff. But no one's interested," he sighed. "It's all died down to a whimper."

He sipped his drink while Horneplush shut one eye

and traced the pattern of the crack in the air with his finger.

"And do you know what I think it is, Horneplush?"

"Eh?" said his friend, who was not paying very much attention.

"I said, do you know what I think it is?"

"Er – rising damp perhaps?"

"What? Rising damp? In pigeons? Don't be daft, man. No, what I think it is, is the *taste*. People seem to be averse to the flavour of the pigeon. They think of pigeons as rats with wings – they've told me so to my face. What balderdash. They're not alike at all. A pigeon tastes completely different from a rat. It's much creamier, for a start." He took another sip and thought for a moment. "Horneplush?"

"Mmm? What, Perry?"

"I was just wondering – have you ever tasted rat?"

Horneplush swizzled the straw around in his glass. "No," he answered. "Can't say I have."

"No, neither have I, now I come to think of it. Although I nibbled a mouse once."

"Really? Where?"

"Just above its tail."

"No, I meant where were you?"

"Ah. It was down Emnobellia way. Jungle territory. I had to get over there to rescue—"

At that moment, the waiter appeared with a small envelope on a silver tray. "Excuse me, Mr Perry," he said quietly, "an urgent telegram from the Valley of the Kings."

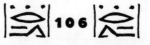

"Eh?" Gerald Ferry put down his Whopper and took the envelope. "Oh," he exclaimed, holding it up to the dim green lamplight. "This'll be from Jim. Perhaps he's found it at last. Thank you, Lucas, that'll be all."

The waiter hovered for baksheesh.

"Oh, Horneplush, be a mate and fix him up, will you?"

"What?" asked Horneplush, his attention diverted from the crack. "Oh, yes, of course." He put twenty piastres onto Lucas's tray. "Here you go."

"Thank you, Mr Horneplush, I will try not to let it change my way of life." He gave a deep nod and disappeared smoothly into the half light at the edge of the room.

"Now, Let's see what we have here," Perry said as he ripped open the envelope. He unfolded the telegram and read it.

"Oh dear," he said when he had finished.

"Not bad news, I hope?"

Gerald Perry frowned and handed Horneplush the piece of paper. "Read for yourself," he muttered.

DISASTER HAS STRUCK STOP UNBELIEVABLE
EXPLOSION STOP SET US BACK MONTHS STOP ALL
WORK WORTH NOTHING STOP MUST START AGAIN
FROM SCRATCH STOP PLEASE ADVISE WE MAY HAVE
EXTENSION POSSIBLY SIX MONTHS OR MORE STOP
WE ARE CLOSE TO M BUT NEED MORE FUNDS TO
BUY MORE TIME STOP WE AWAIT REPLY STOP
SIGNED JIM DORIS BRENDA

Horneplush put down the telegram and raised his eyebrows at his colleague. "Six more months! How ever will you afford it?"

"Oh dear," said Gerald Perry, running the tip of his thumbnail around the edge of his lips. "Oh dear, dear me…"

Brenda stoked the campfire with a stick as she watched Cairo Jim pacing up and down in front of his tent. "Where could she be?" he asked anxiously, his eyes fearful. "Surely we should have had an answer by now."

"It'll come," thought Brenda. "Cairo's a long way away. Be patient."

"It'll come, I suppose," said Jim, scanning the stars for any sign of Doris. "Cairo is a long way away. I must be patient."

"Good thinking," Brenda thought. "And don't worry. It might be good news. Gerald Perry Esquire might give us the money straight away."

"You know, Brenda, I really shouldn't worry. No news is good news, isn't that what they say? Maybe Gerald Perry Esquire will give us the money straight away."

"And then we can get stuck into it again."

"And then we can get stuck into it again."

"After all," the Wonder Camel thought as the flames flickered higher, "we're not the only ones who've had setbacks. Remember that English archaeologist so many years ago? The one who was searching for Tutan Norden? He didn't give up, did he? Not even when his

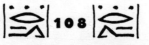

helpers went on strike because they'd run out of marshmallows. No, he soldiered on regardless, and look what *he* found."

Jim stopped pacing and chuckled. "You know, my lovely," he said, "we're not the only ones who've been up against it. Archaeology was never meant to be easy. There was an English chap a long time ago who got into a bit of strife when his helpers walked off the job. They ran out of their marshmallow ration and became disgruntled, so they all packed up and left him. There he was, all by himself, not a soul to help. But he was sure he was close to King Tutan Norden, so what did he do?"

"He kept on digging," thought Brenda.

"He kept on digging, that's what he did. On and on and on. And do you know what he found for all his troubles?"

"Unspeakable treasures."

"Unspeakable treasures, things no one could've ever imagined."

"Marvellous things."

"Marvellous things. The greatest discovery in all Egyptology." Jim clapped his strong hands together once in front of him, loudly and sharply. The sound struck like a bullet into the calm night. "But that, my lovely, will be nothing to what awaits *us*. Nothing indeed. Compared with what we'll find, his discovery will be about as valuable as the contents of a bubblegum machine. The treasure of Martenarten will be far and away the greatest."

That name. Martenarten.

Cairo Jim's eyes filled with dread as he thought of the visitation, detail by chilling detail. Even now he could see that awful thing wrapped in those hideous bandages. He began to tremble at the recollection of that most appalling haze of darkness, which should have harboured eyes, but instead held all the forbidden secrets of the Afterlife. The stench of the thing flooded into his nostrils and made the skin at the back of his knees go clammy, and slimy, and this physical form of his horror slowly spread throughout his entire body, until the archaeologist-poet felt as though he were an enormous slab of Arctic ice.

Bone had been right: Cairo Jim *was* a superstitious man, and this quality was threatening everything Jim, Doris and Brenda had been working towards.

Brenda the Wonder Camel knew she had to take hold of the reins.

"Humans dream," she thought with all her telepathic might. "It happens often. And sometimes the dreams can be so lifelike, it becomes hard to tell them from reality. Think on this, Jim – think of the flicker between a dream and what is real…"

The shadowy flames blinked across his face, and he dwelled on the flicker for the briefest twinkling moment. Then he pushed out his chest and took a deep breath. "What happened yesterday will seem like a bad dream, nothing more," he said to Brenda, smiling. "Perhaps that's all it was, a bad dream. Perhaps we've been working too hard – maybe Doris and I were hallucinating."

"And the explosion? What about that?"

"But the explosion. That was no hallucination. No." He tapped his fingertips together as he thought. "But it could've been some – some underground blast. Yes, that's it. They happen, you know, all the time around the world. Huge build-ups of underground gases. Nowhere to go, so – *boom*. It's all very logical, when you stop to think about it. Why, I reckon—"

He was interrupted by the sound of fluttering wings high above. Doris circled in a wide arc and came swooping down to land at Jim's feet, her beak firmly closed around a small brown envelope. She took it from her beak and handed it to him.

"It's come," she puffed. "I haven't read it yet. The woman at the Post Office kept the place open just for us. Very good of her, I thought."

"People around here are very good," Jim said happily.

"It was sent collect. We owe the Post Office some money next time we go in." Doris slumped exhaustedly against Brenda's humps. "I've had it," she squawked.

"Thank you, my dear," said Jim. "You're a hero."

"Never mind about that," she huffed. "Open it."

"Yes. I suppose I'd better."

But for all his newly found optimism, Cairo Jim was hesitant. He stood there, fingering the envelope. He shook it a few times, and heard the telegram inside

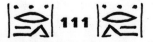

tik-tak back and forth. He held it flat, first in his right hand, then in his left. He tapped it against the palm of his hand. He drew it through his fingers. He examined his name and address printed in Arabic on the front: "Cairo Jim, By the hill shaped like a battered trilby hat, The Valley of the Kings". He licked his lips and dabbed at his perspiring forehead with his handkerchief. He did not want to open it.

"Come on," thought Brenda, fidgeting her hoofs impatiently in the sand. "Tell us."

"Come on," Doris rerked. "Tell us."

He looked at them, their eyes lit up by the flames. Then, his heart pumping like a piston, he tore the thing open. "Here's our answer," he said, unfolding the telegram with shaking fingers. "It's sent from the Old Relics Society."

"Quaaao! Go on."

"Rerk! Go on."

He took a deep breath and read:

SORRY TO HEAR OF DISASTER STOP BUT AFRAID AM NO LONGER IN POSITION TO HELP ANY MORE STOP PIGEONS NOT SELLING AT ALL WELL STOP SUGGEST YOU RETURN TO CAIRO STOP SOCIETY CAN PLACE YOU ON NEW EXPEDITION TO BRAZIL STOP BETTER LUCK NEXT TIME STOP SIGNED GERRY PERRY ESQ

Jim sat down on the sand. He threw the telegram and envelope into the fire and took off his pith helmet.

Doris twitched her wings. "It's not over, is it?"

He looked at her. "What do you mean, Doris?"

"Surely there's something more we can do. Why can't we pool our resources? We still have some money left, don't we?"

Jim emptied the pockets of his Sahara shorts. He opened his wallet and slowly counted the notes inside. "Thirteen pounds," he sighed.

"Is that all?"

"That and a few coins. Hardly enough to get us through a fortnight."

Doris waddled over to him. "What's in this?" she demanded, picking up a small leather pouch with her beak and dropping it in his lap.

He untied the drawstring and tipped out the lapis lazuli brooch which Miss Pyrella Frith had bought from Kelvin Rhampsinites. "Our treasure," he said sadly.

"Reeeerraark! Why don't we sell that? We could go on for a year with what we'd get!"

Jim reached out and ruffled her feathers. "No, my dear, I'm afraid that's right out of the question. You know as well as I, archaeology is an honourable profession. It's a villainous act to sell artefacts such as this. No, this must go to the Museum in Cairo. I'm sure the Director of Antiquities will find a good display case for it."

"I was only trying to help—"

"Thank you."

He put it back into the pouch and tied it securely.

Then he stood and put on his helmet. "I think we should turn in, my friends. We'll have to be up early in the morning. There's a lot of packing to do."

"Tomorrow?" gasped Doris. "We leave tomorrow?"

"There's no sense putting it off any longer than we have to. I'll go over to Luxor and arrange a felucca. We can say goodbye to Mrs Amun-Ra and Miss Frith on the way. A few days on the Nile and we'll be – we'll be—"

He could not continue, the lump in his throat was too big. He swallowed hard.

"Jim—" Doris began.

"It's all right, my dear. Goodnight. And thank you both, from the very bottom of my heart, for all your efforts." He turned and went to his tent.

Doris scratched around, not knowing what to do or say. After a while, she decided the best thing would be to go to her perch. She looked at Brenda and noticed the Wonder Camel's nostrils quivering.

"Men must endure their going hence, even as their coming hither," the macaw said gently. "Ripeness is all."

"And that's true, too," thought Brenda with a snort.

"Goodnight, you Wonderful silent thing," Doris said. "You'll be sorely missed." And she flew over and gave her a quick peck on the ear before gliding away.

The Wonder Camel's sadness was almost as great as Jim's, for she knew there was no place for her in Cairo.

In one of her large eyes, an enormous tear welled. It rolled down her cheek and splashed onto the sand, where for a brief moment it formed a little pool.

Then the fine grains absorbed it, and the ground once again became as dry as dust.

BRAVO, BRENDA
THE WONDER CAMEL

LONG AGO, a giant palm tree grew in the Valley. It was the tallest of its kind, its trunk thicker than any other, and the huge fronds which sprouted from the top of it were luxuriant and green. When the weather was extremely hot, men, women, children and camels were known to come and rest in the cool shadow it cast over the sand.

It was the only tree, indeed, the only piece of greenery, in the whole Valley. Nobody was quite sure how it survived. Water in this place, both above and beneath the ground, was scarce at the best of times; at the worst of times, it was non-existent. A person could die of thirst here if they were ill-prepared. But somehow this tree had continued to grow and flourish, every year pushing farther and farther up towards the blazing sun.

It had stood for many centuries, and during that time had witnessed much. It had watched, towering and silent, as dozens of royal funeral processions had entered the Valley to place the Kings in their richly furnished tombs from where they would leave this world and be spirited away into the After Life. It had seen the hordes of desperate tomb robbers creeping through the sandhills after nightfall, their carts trundling across the desert, ready to be loaded with all the gold they could carry. It had heard the bloodcurdling cries of countless jackals howling into the night, had withstood being blown by fierce dust storms, had been the roosting place for thousands of generations of bird families, and had had graffiti carved into its trunk by naughty youths and explorers.

Then, over a thousand years ago, it began to die. Its leaves withered and shrank, turning from green to brown until they were brittle enough to be burnt to nothing by the sun. Its gigantic trunk started to rot slowly from the inside, and gradually this most majestic of palms became nothing more than a giant cylinder of papery wood.

It stood like that until one day, when the heat was unbearably harsh, it caught on fire. The flames lasted for a day and a night. And all that remained of the once awesome plant was a pile of ash. Its fragments were soon scattered over the Valley by the strong desert winds.

The tree had been famous for miles around and when it had gone, the sense of loss was great. The people who lived in nearby Gurna village and across the Nile in Luxor felt as though they had lost a member of their family. The High Priests from the Temple of Karnak could not explain its mysterious demise; they thought it might be an omen of bad things to come, such as the death of a King or Queen.

The story of the tree was passed down from mother

to daughter and from father to son, who in turn told it to their children, who then told it to the next generation. Gradually, though, the story began to shorten. A father would say to his son, "Once, my son, there was a mighty tree in this place, so tall that you could not see the top of it." When that son himself became a father, he would tell his daughter, "Once, my daughter, there was a tree in this place, so tall," and he would raise his hand to the sky. Then, years later, that daughter would say to her own daughter, "Once, my daughter, there was a tree here, a tall tree," but she would not raise her hand. The story became so brief that when children heard it, it meant nothing at all, and they did not remember it. And so they had nothing to tell their children. Thus the legend of the tree, like the tree itself, became nothing.

But all of that was a long time ago.

Now it is early morning. The sun is only just rising over the Valley, the light beginning to turn from deep night blue to harsh orange. In a few hours it will be white, bright, almost blinding, and another day will happen.

For Brenda the Wonder Camel, it was the saddest morning she had known. Soon Jim would be up, and he and Doris would set about packing their belongings and making the arrangements for their journey to Cairo. She had thought about this all night and, dreading the morrow, she had not been able to sleep.

"It's unfair," she thought as she wandered around

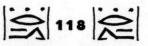

near the dig, "especially after all their hard work. They should stay and keep searching. Martenarten *must* be here somewhere." She snorted loudly and scraped a hoof through the dust. "What we need," she wished, "is a miracle. Right now, right this very morning, before it's too late." But, despite being an optimistic camel, Brenda knew deep down in her humps that miracles didn't happen any more. Not in this day and age.

She lumbered away from the mess of rubble which had made the entrance to the dig impassable, and turned her head to spit. It was then that her eye spotted something in the sand.

"That's strange," she thought. "I've not noticed that before. Hmm. I wonder what it is."

Screwing up her nose, she crept towards it, not quite certain if it were friend or foe. If it were alive, she didn't want to scare it. It might be something delicious, after all. But the nearer she came to it, the less alive it appeared. It was absolutely still. "It might be sleeping," thought Brenda. "Maybe it's fallen asleep and tucked its small head underneath its arm. I must be quiet."

She stooped and looked closely. "Goodness, how wrinkled. And what an unfetching colour – all sort of brown and grey and sandy. Not a patch on my elegant camel hues. Hmmm. And what an odd shape." She inched closer. "No," she decided, "it's not asleep. I would see some part of it breathing if it were. When Doris sleeps, her chest goes up and down, like little noiseless tremors in the earth. Hmmmm. What *is* this thing? I've never seen the like of it in the Valley."

The puzzle of the Wrinkled Thing annoyed her, for she was the sort of creature who had to have a reason for everything, whether it was animal, vegetable or mineral. She screwed up her brows and had a quick chew on her tongue as she decided on a plan of action. Then, her hoofs poised for springing, she took a short run-off and leapt onto it.

Nothing. No squeak came from it as it lay beneath her hoof. It made no "splat" noise. It didn't try to get away. It just sat there as it had done when she had been observing it.

Tentatively, she raised her hoof and noticed for the first time that the thing was not on the sand, but was partially buried. She took a step back and lowered her head until her nostrils were touching its coarse surface. If she sniffed it, she might get a clue.

"Ssssnnniiiifff."

All at once she sneezed violently and shook her head. Dust. It smelled of nothing but dust and age. A forgotten smell, she thought. She gave it a kick and heard a wooden sound clacking against her hoof. And she realised what it was.

Only a root. An old dead root, gnarled and wizened, from some long-forgotten tree.

Disappointed that it was nothing more exciting, she snorted loudly and bared her teeth. Down went her head and her jaws locked around it. "I'll have this thing," she thought. "Why should it be allowed to stay

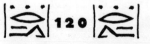

here when Doris and Jim have to go? Hrrmmph!"

She gave a small tug, but it was steadfast and would not budge. Brenda scowled. Getting a better grip (and being careful not to breathe – sneezing was a thing she did not enjoy, it made her humps ache), she had another go. This time she pulled harder, moving her head back and forth as she did so. The root began to loosen. She pulled even harder. Small clods of earth around the root dislodged and crumbled away from it. "Aha," she thought. "Now we're getting somewhere." The next tug, more forceful than the others, caused the root to start coming up out of the ground. It was longer than she had imagined; it seemed to go to the very centre of the earth. She pulled and pulled and more of the long knotty thing came free.

Finally she gave a terrific yank with her strong Wonder Camel jaws, and it was out.

She reeled backwards, tumbling head over hoofs with it in her mouth, as the ground where it had been planted collapsed with a mighty roar.

Crrrrrrrraaaaaaaassssssssshhhhhhhh!

The noise was almost as loud as the explosion had been, and all the ground in all the Valleys shook with a low rumble.

Over in Gurna, Mrs Amun-Ra woke up to the sound of her crockery rattling in the cupboard. A few streets away, in Miss Pyrella Frith's darkroom, the bottles of developing fluid and sunscreen lotion and undiluted insect repellent jiggled on their shelves. In the pastures,

the cows of the Hapi family awoke with a start from their peaceful sleep, their udders swinging in alarm. Abdullah Rhampsinites, in the middle of a dreadful nightmare in which he was being carried off by a giant budgerigar, opened his eye and screamed. The noise woke Kelvin, who was sleeping next to him, and he screamed too, so Abdullah pinched him hard on the arm. People jumped from their beds and dived underneath them, thinking an earthquake had struck.

Cairo Jim came rushing from his tent, Doris flying close by his head.

"Rark!" cried the macaw. "What on earth—?"

Jim raised his binoculars to his sun-spectacles and directed them at the dig. He focused in on Brenda. There she was, lying in a dazed state on the ground. In her mouth was a long spindly root.

"Brenda!" he shouted. "Come on, Doris."

She clasped onto his shoulder and off they pelted.

"Quaaaaaooooo," snorted the Wonder Camel, her head spinning. "From now on I'll stick to worms," she resolved.

"Brenda, my lovely!" Jim shouted from across the gaping hole, which lay in a one-hundred-and-eighty-degree line away from the dig.

She raised a hoof and gave them a stunned wave.

"What happened?"

She stood groggily and shrugged.

Doris jumped from Jim's shoulder and waddled to the edge of the hole. "Jim," she gasped, peering down, "look at this!"

"Well, I'll be swoggled!" he exclaimed, tilting his pith helmet forward and scratching the back of his neck.

There below them, set into the underground rock and lit only by the pale morning sunlight, was the tip of a door.

An ancient Egyptian Door of Death.

▲▲▲▲▲ 9 ▲▲▲▲▲

THE ACCIDENTAL ARCHAEOLOGIST

ONLY THE TOP PART of the Door was visible; the remainder had been buried by the fall of rock and sand.

Jim and Doris stood staring down at it for a long time, both unable to speak. Brenda shook her head around and around until she regained her senses. Then she came closer and poked her head over the hole. When she saw what was below, she did a little dance on the sand.

The heart of Cairo Jim beat quickly. His mouth went dry, his legs felt hollow and unsteady, and the palms of his hands started to drip with excitement. He knelt down on all fours and craned his head over the edge. The hole was wide enough for him and Doris to enter, and he calculated that there was enough room at the bottom to swing an axe or sledgehammer. He dug his fingernails into the edge and leaned farther, but as he looked, his eyes wide behind his sun-spectacles, his pith helmet toppled over his forehead and plummeted into the pit.

For ten long seconds they watched it fall. Then they heard a faint "plop" as it landed on the soft sand at the bottom.

Jim crawled back from the edge. "Right," he said to

Doris and Brenda, "Let's get to work."

"Rark!" said Doris eagerly.

In no time at all they had fetched the necessary equipment: one long coil of rope, Jim's best lamp, a rope ladder, the axe and sledgehammer, a small but powerful battery-operated torch, several brushes, the compass and sextant, a medium-sized pick, two shovels (one large, the other smaller), notepaper and pencils, magnifying glass, matches and a box of candles, binoculars and pocket-knife.

Jim added his umbrella to the pile of equipment. It had accompanied him on all his discoveries, and he now took it along more out of superstition than for practical reasons; it gave him a feeling of protection and he did not like to be without it.

"How about these?" asked Doris, slipping her pack of cards into the knapsack.

"No, Doris," said Jim, taking them out. "We won't have time."

So she busied herself with filling Jim's water bottle, while Brenda found her way around to the other side of the hole.

When Jim had tucked everything into his belt, pockets and knapsack, he began to unwind the rope. He gave one end of it to Brenda.

"My lovely," he said to her, "Doris and I are going in. There's not enough room for you, I'm afraid."

She raised her eyebrows in disappointment.

"But that's for the best. We need you here."

She raised her eyebrows higher, this time with curiosity.

"We need you to hold this firmly, more firmly than you've ever held anything before. It's a long way down. One slip and we're gone."

Brenda took the rope in her mouth and cemented her jaws around it. She gave a single snort and nodded. Now she felt important.

"That's the way," said Jim. He threw the other end into the hole. The three of them waited while it travelled to the bottom, listening as it unwound and bumped against the wall of rock on its way down.

Jim scratched his stubbled chin. "Ready, Doris my dear?"

"Too right."

He reached down, offering his hand. She put her wing into it.

"Up you come, then." He lifted her onto his shoulder and she folded her wing around his neck.

"Keep guard, Brenda," he said as he grabbed the rope and hoisted himself and Doris over the edge.

"Too right," snorted the Wonder Camel.

Jim paused at the brink and, clinging to the rope, looked into the early sky. "This one's for Jocelyn," he thought, "wherever she is."

He took a deep breath and they disappeared slowly into the earth.

They descended cautiously, Brenda all the while taking the strain high above. Jim let the rope pass

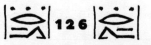

carefully through his hands after having felt around with his boot for decent footholds. He was weighed down considerably, and this made their journey all the more cumbersome.

When they were near the bottom, Doris flew from his shoulder and went to nestle on top of the fallen pith helmet. Jim jumped the last metre and landed on his feet.

"We're here, Brenda," he shouted. "So far, so good. Pull it up."

Brenda started to haul the rope back up. When she had all of it above ground again, she wound it into a neat coil and sat next to it, settling herself for a patient wait.

Jim dumped the equipment into a corner. The light had become stronger as the sun had risen higher, and a single diagonal shaft lit up the top of the Door, its beam yellow and glimmering.

"Well," he breathed, taking the magnifying glass from his knapsack, "let's take a look." He crouched down in front of the Door.

Doris fluttered over beside him and watched as his huge eye moved slowly along the surface. He put the glass into his shirt pocket and ran his hand along the perfectly straight-lined recesses carved into the Door.

A broad smile spread across his face. "I haven't seen one of these in a long, long time," he said quietly.

Doris could tell he was becoming excited. She bent forward and rapped the Door sharply with her beak.

A hollow echo reverberated from the other side. The noise of the single rap pulsed back and back, and farther back still, until it became dull and far off in the distance. Then it died away to nothing.

"It's wooden," she said. "Cedar, I think."

"Doris!" Jim whispered.

"What?"

"Do that again."

"Do what again?"

"Tap it."

She did so. Once again, the echo followed, tap, tap, tap, on and away, bursting through time as it bounced around in the unseen void on the other side.

Cairo Jim's arms and legs erupted with goosebumps.

"Did you hear it?" he asked anxiously. "Did you hear?"

"Rerark. What of it?"

"The most wonderful sound in all archaeology!"

"What do you mean?"

He scooped her up and held her close to his face. "My dear, that echo."

"What of it?"

"That echo tells us two things. Two things that make all the difference between everything and nothing at all."

"Really?"

"You bet your sun-spectacles it does. The fact that we can hear an echo means firstly that something lies beyond. If there were nothing there, if it were all rock and sand, we wouldn't hear a thing."

Still crouching, he stomped one foot on the ground. A dull, muffled thud rose with the small cloud of dust.

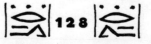

"*That's* what we'd hear if it were solid behind – the Egyptians often built False Doors to throw tomb robbers off the track. But this isn't artificial. No, this is as real as the day I was born!"

The plumes on Doris's head stiffened and arched forward. "And the second thing?" she asked, her beak hardly able to spit out the words. "What's that?"

The goosebumps on Jim's arms and legs multiplied, until he had pyramids of goosebumps. He held the macaw even closer as he spoke in a barely audible voice.

"That, my dear, is the most important clue of all." He paused to lick his lips. "We can only see a small part of this Door. Look," he said, turning her around. "The part that hasn't been buried is only a fraction of the total thing. It's only just big enough for a grown man to crawl on his stomach through to the other side. After we've broken through it, that is. The rest of it could go down beneath the sand for one metre or for twenty. There's no way to tell, unless we dig all this away. But we *can* tell something about it, thanks to the echo."

Doris cocked her head towards him. "What?"

Jim spoke slowly, as though he was measuring every word he was about to speak. "Doris, if this Door were not intact beneath this sand, there would be no way the sound waves could carry as far back as they do. The resonance of the echo would be flatter, if there were any echo at all. That noise, my friend, means the most important thing of all. It means," and here he raised his voice, for this was the best thing an archaeologist could ever hope to find, "it means that this Door has never been violated. Never opened. Never broken down. What lies beyond has *never been disturbed*!"

Doris jumped from his grasp and hopped around on the compacted sand. She felt as if all her birddays had come at once. "Rark!" she screeched. "Reek! Rerk! Whacko!"

"Whacko, indeed," said Jim.

She stopped in mid-hop and turned to him. "What are we waiting for, then?"

Jim stood and went to retrieve his pith helmet. "Let's get to work, my dear. A Discovery awaits us."

He took the axe and, pausing only to spit onto his palms, began to hack away at the Door. Hefty thwacks followed one after the other. Being ancient and dry, the timber splintered away easily and after a dozen blows, Jim had smashed enough of a hole for him to slide through.

"There," he puffed. "That wasn't hard, was it?"

Doris delved into the knapsack and found the torch. "Let's take a look," she said.

The archaeologist-poet lay on his stomach and took off his sun-spectacles. He extended his neck and pushed his head through the opening, as did Doris.

On the other side, all was dark and gloomy. Doris's torchlight picked out a mass of cobwebs, a canopy of intricate and dense gossamer which made it impossible to see very far into the distance.

"Erk," she shuddered. "I hate those things."

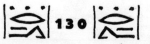

"There's nothing to be afraid of," soothed Jim. "Chances are, the spiders who wove them are long gone. Here, my dear, shine the light downwards. Let's see what the drop is."

Doris obeyed and together they estimated it was about five metres to the floor.

"We'll need the rope ladder," Jim decided. He stood and pulled it from his belt. Undoing the fastening rope, he let the ladder fall into the chamber. Then he attached the end he was holding to a large rock at the entrance. When he was satisfied it was secure, he knelt and raised the knapsack to his shoulder.

"Come on, Doris," he whispered. "And be careful. Stay close to me at all times. We don't know what's in there."

He lay on the ground and, pushing his legs through the hole, proceeded to find his footing on the ladder.

"Jim?"

"What, my dear?"

"Is this – could this be – Martenarten?"

He stopped and looked at her, his eyes uncertain. "There are hundreds of undiscovered tombs in the Valley. I really don't know." Suddenly he flashed her a huge, hopeful smile. "But there's only one way to find out. All aboard!"

She jumped onto his shoulder and down they climbed.

The umbrella, lamp, axe, sledgehammer, shovels and pick knocked against each other as they swung from

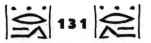

Jim's wide belt. Doris still held the torch firmly under her right wing, and every time Jim stepped onto another rung, the torchlight bobbed wildly up and down, illuminating the cobwebs one second and the dark walls the next.

Halfway down, he stopped. "Ouch."

"What's wrong?" asked Doris.

"The umbrella. It's being a nuisance." He reached down, the ladder swaying when he took one hand from it, and disengaged the offending article. "That's better. Let's see how far it is now," he said, and let the umbrella drop from his grasp.

A few seconds passed, long and silent, as the umbrella was swallowed into the darkness. There was a loud clatter.

"Aha," Jim smiled. "Just as I'd hoped." He turned his head to Doris. "The floor is paved."

She cooed quietly and they continued down.

Down …

    down …

        down …

           down to the blackened depths,

until at last the ladder came to an end, and the boots of Cairo Jim stepped onto the paving stones.

Turning around, they were confronted close-up by the wall of cobwebs, the silky patterns in them heavily smothered in the fine white dust of many ages past.

Jim swung his knapsack to the floor and released the lamp. "Could you light this please, Doris? I have

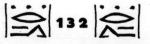

some house-cleaning to do."

"Be my guest," grimaced the macaw. She sprang to the knapsack to find the matches, while Jim pulled all the larger tools from his belt and leaned them against the Door. This side of it was not carved like the other and, as he observed that it had not been smashed in any way, a small thrill raced through his veins. He had been right.

He selected the big shovel and held it straight out in front of his body. Then he started to batter away at the cobwebs. They were thick and firm, but for this archaeologist, undaunting; he had seen many such structures in his years of experience, and he now regarded them not as an obstacle but as part and parcel of antiquity.

Soon they were cleared and the shovel resembled a huge stick of white candyfloss. He put it down just as Doris lit the lamp.

The bronze-coloured lamplight glowed and flickered. For the first time, they were able to see the gallery in all its entirety.

It was vast, the biggest Cairo Jim had ever seen. He picked up the lamp and held it high. The ceiling at this end must have been at least ten metres tall. Doris took the torch and moved its beam slowly towards the far wall. As the light travelled along the rough ceiling, they observed the incline. At the opposite end, the distance from ceiling to floor appeared to be twice that of where they were standing.

Doris gasped.

She directed the beam down the opposite wall. Here

they saw another Door of Death, this one almost twenty metres high. It appeared to be carved of granite, for dozens of tiny rock minerals twinkled in the light. The floor beneath it was much lower than where Jim and Doris were; it slanted away from them at such a steep angle that if they had dropped a ball it would have rolled quickly down to the granite Door.

Both walls at the sides of the gallery were covered with detailed carvings painted in all the colours of the rainbow. A hunting scene on the left wall was so clear and bright, it might have been painted yesterday. A line of men was stalking animals in a field. The hunters carried spears and knives, wore short skirts and had bald heads. The next panel showed lots of brightly coloured animals – lions, elephants, tigers, giraffes, birds of great beauty, jackals, Emnobellian Jungle Donkeys, crocodiles, even monkeys. None of the animals looked at all pleased.

On the right wall, some kind of procession was depicted. Lines of slaves were carrying cages mounted on long thin poles. Inside the cages were lions, elephants, tigers, a giraffe (that was the tallest cage), birds of great but sad beauty, jackals and crocodiles. Several Emnobellian Jungle Donkeys were being ridden in front of the procession, and a dwarf led three monkeys on a chain. The animals on this wall looked very unhappy.

The procession was followed by a group of richly clothed men whose skin was darker than the slaves'.

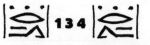

They carried small boxes decorated with jewels and ivory.

"Nubians and Abyssinians," Jim told Doris. "They've come with gifts for the King or Queen. Probably for a coronation."

"Coo," cooed Doris. "Let's see more."

She took a step forward, and would have taken another, but Jim reached out and grabbed her.

"No!" he hissed. "No, you mustn't."

She flapped her wings, trying to break free. "What? Why not?"

"Settle down, Doris. All is not what it appears."

"Eh?"

He put down the lamp and took the torch from her.

"Look," he said, pointing it at the ceiling. "See how it's so uneven? All those huge grooves spaced along?"

"So? The workers got a little messy. So what?"

"Ah, no, my dear, not messy. *Clever.* Those are traps."

"Traps?"

"Booby traps. I've been in tombs like this before. Over in the Valley of the Nobles there's a tomb which had traps almost identical to these. They were released long ago, nobody knows how or by whom, and now the grooves in the ceiling are empty. I made a special study of those traps one summer when I was at archaeology school."

"Rark."

"If we're not careful, all these will be triggered off

too, and we'll be entombed."

"Entombed?"

"Sealed in alive." Doris gulped.

"But there is a way around it," Jim said. "And it all depends on you."

"M–me?"

"You." He tapped his lower lip with his finger. "We have to get to the other Door, That's for certain. What we want is on the other side of it. But the ancient Egyptians constructed this chamber so that the slightest disturbance of air in here – the smallest flutter of a bird's wing, for example, in the centre of the space – will release the traps."

"Terrific," said Doris, wishing right now that she was back at Mrs Amun-Ra's tea-rooms, stuffing her beak with shergolds. "What happens then?"

"Then, if I'm not mistaken, huge slabs of rock will descend slowly from those grooves."

"Erk."

"There's no way we can take more than five steps without activating those traps," Jim said slowly. "Whether we like it or not, those slabs are going to descend. There's no avoiding it. It's only a matter of time before they reach the floor. But we can use time, Doris. For once, it can be on our side, instead of against us." He turned to her. "You, my dear, can stop them before they reach the ground."

"Me? How?"

"I'll show you." He took his binoculars and looked

far down the shaft to the granite Door, at the same time shining the torch on it. "Good."

"What's good?"

"Take a look."

He gave her the binoculars and she looked carefully. "I don't see anything."

"Concentrate."

She scrunched her eyes. Then something appeared. A pattern of small holes dotted the centre of the Door, each of them about the size of a human's little finger.

"Holes," she said. "I see holes."

"One of which you can use to save us, my dear." She put down the binoculars and looked at him in a puzzled manner.

"One of those holes holds the secret," he explained. "If we wedge something in the correct one, the traps will stop automatically, and the slabs of rock will stay where they are, dead in their tracks. Then we can still get in and out, but only if we manage to stop the slabs with enough room left between them and the floor."

"Why does it depend on me?"

"My dear, it's of the utmost importance that we get to those holes in the shortest possible time. Every second will count. It'd take me a full two minutes to find my way down this darkened ramp, two minutes in which those slabs would start coming down, and even then I'd be running as fast as I could."

"Raark! Too dangerous!" cried the macaw. "One slip down there and you'd break your neck."

"Exactly. The floor is too uneven. But the air, on the other hand, is smooth, and free from any obstacles."

"I see," she prowked. "That's where I come in. I fly, yes?"

Jim nodded. "As fast as you can. Everything depends on it. If I shine the torch at the holes from here, you should be able to see them without too much difficulty."

"What will I use to block the hole?" she asked.

"Good question," replied Jim. He looked around at the equipment as he thought. Suddenly his eyes lit up. "Of course!" He grabbed the umbrella and gave it to her. "The pointed end will be just the thing."

"I knew this'd come in handy some day," Doris squawked.

"Ram it in, good and hard, until you hit the correct hole."

"Roger."

"If it looks too dicey, if the slabs are getting too close to the floor, I'll give you a shout to come back. We don't want you trapped."

"Jim?"

"What, my dear?"

"One question: which is the correct hole?"

He hesitated, then said, "I don't know, my friend. That varies from tomb to tomb. You'll have to keep trying till you find it."

"Why are there so many?"

He put his hand on her shoulder and spoke calmly. "I didn't want to tell you this, Doris, but one of those

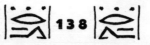

holes is deadly. It's attached to some kind of release mechanism deep inside the Door. It was the same in the tomb I studied at archaeology school. If you choose it by mistake, the traps will come crashing down, and the whole place will collapse."

"Whoops," said Doris nervously.

"Unfortunately there's no way to tell which one it is."

"Uh-oh," she muttered.

He ruffled her feathers. "If I had wings," he told her, "I'd do this myself. I hate putting the both of us at risk. Are you sure you want to go through with it?"

She puffed out her chest feathers and put the umbrella over her shoulder. "The gods be good to us," she grinned stoically. "Bid me farewell, and smile."

Jim grinned back. "Shakespeare?"

"You bet your sock-garters. See you at the other end."

She took a huge breath and crossed her claws. Then she flapped up into the air, the umbrella in her beak, and shot off like a bullet into the darkened chamber.

Halfway along, she stopped and hovered. She looked up at the grooves. "Jim," she called, the umbrella making it a bit difficult for her to speak clearly.

"What, Doris?" he shouted back. "Why have you stopped?"

She let out a stifled giggle. "I think you were wrong. It doesn't look like anything's going to—"

That was as far as she got. At that precise instant there was a violent shuddering of the ceiling, followed

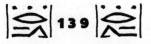

by an appalling scrunching sound which burst from somewhere high above.

Four gigantic slabs of solid granite emerged through the wide grooves and began to descend. Slowly they came towards her, down and onwards with a long drawn-out crunch of rock and earth. Doris nearly swallowed the umbrella.

"My apologies," she screeched.

"Fly!" Jim yelled at the top of his lungs. "Go on, my dear, *fly!*"

She took off, the noise building as the slabs pushed down.

Jim grabbed the torch and shone it at the holes far away in the distance. Doris flew on, faster than she had ever flown.

"I'm here," she shouted back after what seemed like a hundred years.

"Can you see the holes all right?"

She pulled the umbrella from her beak and hovered with her one free wing. "That's fine. There's six of them, Jim."

"Six?"

The slabs were now a metre out of the grooves and still descending.

"Choose one now," Jim yelled.

Doris paused as she made her choice. "Eeny, meeny, miny – mo!" With all her might, she rammed the pointed end into the hole third from the left. The umbrella stuck straight out from the Door.

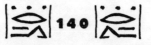

Nothing happened. The slabs kept coming.

"Try another," shouted Jim, watching through the binoculars.

She grasped the umbrella and yanked it out. "Now, Let's see – what about this one?" Once again, she rammed it, this time into the hole at the far left-hand side.

Once again, nothing. The noise was becoming louder and small fragments of rock were falling from the ceiling.

"Try the one on the extreme right!" Jim yelled above the din.

Out came the umbrella. Doris was beginning to feel butterflies in her stomach now – the slabs were nearly three metres out of the ceiling. She whipped it into the hole Jim had suggested.

To no effect. Onwards they came, seemingly unstoppable in their course.

Wrenching the umbrella out, she decided to go for the hole next to it. She clenched the thing in her beak and flew a little distance away from the Door, as much as the slab nearest it would allow her. Then she made a flying assault on the hole.

The umbrella went straight into it, the silver pointed end buried to its hilt. Doris reeled from the impact.

Still, nothing. The slabs kept coming down and down. They had now descended into more than half the chamber, and Jim had to kneel on all fours to shine the light underneath them.

"Doris! They're moving faster! Hurry!"

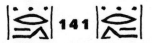

She shook her head and attached herself to the umbrella, but when she tried to pull it out, it wouldn't come. It was wedged fast. In her enthusiasm, she had jammed it in too hard.

"Jim!" she screeched. "It's stuck!"

"What?"

"The umbrella. I can't get it out. It won't move!"

Cairo Jim went pale. In another minute, the gallery would be shut off, and whatever lay on the other side of the granite Door would be lost to them. There was not enough time for him to scramble underneath the slabs to have a go at the umbrella himself.

In that awful moment, he made a decision:

"Doris! You'll have to come back. Leave the umbrella. Fly back now, and you'll be saved."

There was no reply. He tried to see her in the distance, but the slabs prevented it.

"Doris!" he shouted as he watched them approaching the floor. "Did you hear me?"

"Raaaaaark! No way. We've come too far!"

She summoned up all her strength and gripped the umbrella. With an enormous grunt, she took the strain. Then she leaned backwards and pulled.

Once.

Twice.

Three times.

There was a sharp scraping noise and the umbrella came free, forcing her back with the effort.

"It's out," she squawked.

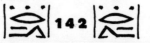

"Doris! Come back!"

But she didn't hear him; the noise from the traps had built to a deafening crescendo.

There was no time to waste. The lower the slabs came, the more they cut off the light from Jim's torch. Second by second, the Door was growing darker and darker...

Now, Doris had a terrible choice to make. Two holes remained untried. One of them would stop the traps, but the other...

As this thought crashed through her mind, she began to perspire. The drops of moisture rolled down from her feathered forehead and dripped off her beak. She looked at the two holes, their black roundness staring at her like eyes from the After Life.

Her wings became slippery with anxiety and, before she knew it, the umbrella slid from her grip and fell to the dark floor.

"Oh, no!" she screamed.

She turned around and saw the torch light shafting through from under the slabs. There was now only a metre and a half between them and the floor.

In desperation, she swooped down and rummaged on the dark paving stones. She kicked her feet this way and that; she brushed her wings along the stones; she poked her beak into the darkness. At last she felt something hard, something which was not dusty or sandy. Something long and curved at one end. An umbrella can be a joyous thing at times.

She grabbed it with her beak and swept up into the blackness, to where she thought the holes were. Running her wing over the Door, she found them. Quickly she counted them all until she felt sure she had pinpointed the holes second from the left and third from the right. The last remaining ones.

Without pausing to think about her drenched feathers or the consequence of what would happen if she took the wrong one, she whacked the umbrella in, hard and fast.

Into the hole third from the right.

There was a huge shuddering of the ceiling, and time almost

stopped.

The slabs came to a grinding halt, less than a metre from the floor. And all was quiet.

"Well, what do you know?" she chuckled, hardly able to believe it.

"Doris! My dear, you've done it!" Jim called, scarcely able to contain himself.

"*We've* done it," she replied, fluttering to the floor and shaking out her feathers.

"Wait there, I'm coming through."

He collected all the equipment into a bundle and crawled down the sloping floor, being careful not to bang his pith helmet on the bottom of the slabs. He held the torch firmly in his mouth to light the way.

A few minutes later, he was with his friend.

Placing the torch on the ground, he scooped her up

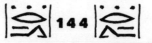

144

and gave her an enormous hug. Then he tousled her plumage and said:

> When everything looked dark and dim,
> those slabs almost to floor,
> you saved it all. For Cairo Jim,
> you are the best macaw!

"Raaark," said Doris, "this is no time for poetry. Let's get on with it."

"Right you are," Jim laughed. "Let's do just that."

They busied themselves with the lamp and torch and found the Door to be as solid as the rock from which it was made. "It's probably half a metre thick, if I know those ancient Egyptians," said Jim. "The quickest way to get through it would be to dynamite, but that's far too risky. The whole place would cave in on top of us. No, there's nothing for it but the sledgehammer and pick."

Doris flew up with the lamp and perched carefully on the umbrella as Jim began to work furiously at the base of the Door. Firstly he used the sledgehammer to bombard it with a barrage of savage blows, one on top of the other, all on the same section of granite. The sound cracked out again and again into the eerie darkness.

For nearly twenty minutes he went on like this. Then at last the rock began to crack. Small hairline fractures appeared, their outlines faint in the flickering light. Jim continued the attack, his blows becoming stronger and stronger. All through his work he kept check on Doris and the umbrella.

Soon the cracks enlarged and spread and small pieces of rock began to crumble and fall away in powdery fragments.

It was now time for the pick. He took it up and with swift strokes started to hack into the weakened granite. "Tikk, tikk, tikk," pinged the tool as it struck the surface. Sometimes a particularly well-placed blow would dislodge large chunks of the Door; at other times only small splinters of felspar or quartz would fly out, twinkling as they caught the light. But Cairo Jim carried on without pause, the sweat building on his brow and trickling down his back, his lungs full of the musty air of this subterranean gallery.

After an hour, he had opened up enough of a gap for them to enter. He dropped the pick at his feet and wiped the caked-on dust from his forehead.

"Right," he puffed, reaching into the knapsack for his water bottle, "you can come down now, my dear." Carefully Doris removed the lamp from the umbrella and brought it down to the floor.

Jim opened the bottle and took a huge swig of the cold water, feeling it flow down his throat and into his chest, quenching the raging thirst that had built from his efforts. He screwed the lid back on and wiped his mouth with the back of his hand.

"Well, Doris, shall we go?"

"I thought you'd never ask."

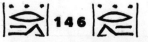

"Remember, stay close."

They shone their lights into the gap and slowly squeezed themselves and all their tools through it.

As one, Cairo Jim and Doris gasped. On the other side of that Door of Death they saw a vast underground temple, the length and breadth of four football fields.

They had seen many temples before, both above and beneath the ground, but none like this. The dark space in front of them was a labyrinth. The gloom was filled with a forest of polished limestone columns, each so wide in girth that three fully grown men who were so inclined could not join hands around it. The columns were all beautifully carved with ornate scenes and hieroglyphs. Jim shone his torch over several and watched breathlessly as the beam travelled slowly up and up until it reached the ceiling. Nets of cobwebbing joined their tops to the roof.

Doris had waddled off to poke about in a small pile of pebbles which she hoped might conceal a stash of rubies.

Jim stood and shut his eyes. He imagined himself back in time until he was standing in this very temple three thousand years ago.

He saw small bowls of fire lighting the walls, the flames licking away at the darkness. He saw a procession of High Priests approaching, all of them swinging low-hanging vessels of burning incense in front of their holy robes. Behind them through the smoke came the Vestal Virgins, chanting in voices like honey. Then another series of voices: lower, deeper, the chanting turning into a dirge as the members of the Royal Court made their way into this hallowed place. And then at last the Pharaoh appeared, borne aloft on a golden throne mounted on gilt poles, carried by a dozen slaves.

Cairo Jim opened his eyes at this point in the imaginary procession. Somehow he could not picture the Pharaoh, try as he might. He found himself seeing only a black fuzz at that moment of his dream. All he could hear now was the faint scratching of Doris's beak against the limestone floor and small pebbles being shifted.

He moved the torchlight across the tops of the columns, over the cobwebs which seemed to be sticking them to the ceiling. And there, showing faintly through the cobwebs, was a painting.

Silver in colour, crescent in shape.

Next to it was another, next to that another; and so the pattern continued.

He flashed the torch wildly across the temple ceiling. It was covered in these designs. Hundreds and thousands of them.

"Ta Ra Ra Boom De Ay," he uttered quietly.

Doris lifted her head from her pebbles. "What?"

"Ta Ra Ra Boom De Ay." He was transfixed by the sight.

Doris looked up at the roving beam of light. When she saw the myriad of moons, all of them painted in the silver moon-paint that had made the High Priests so

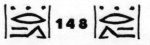 148

poor, she almost fell backwards. "Ta Ra Ra Boom De Ay," she crooned.

The archaeologist and the macaw looked at each other. "Martenarten," they whispered in unison.

Meanwhile, high above and slightly to the left, Brenda the Wonder Camel stirred drowsily. She blinked and looked up at the sun, which had now risen to its midmorning point in the sky.

"Hmm," she thought, "they've been a long time down there. I wonder what they're doing? Fossicking around, I suppose." Lazily she swatted at a fly with her tail. "I hope they're all right."

There was a noise then, only small, but a noise nonetheless. It came from somewhere behind her.

"What's that?" she wondered.

She turned her head to look, but seeing nothing, gave a snort and returned to her daydreams. How she wished she had a good Western right now.

In the Temple of Martenarten, Cairo Jim and Doris were dancing. Around and around in little circles they gambolled, in and out of the columns, Jim clapping his hands together and Doris swinging her hips in time to the beat.

"Martenarten, Martenarten, Martenarten," Jim sang loudly.

"Rark, rark, rark," joined in Doris.

"Ta Ra Ra Boom De Ay," they sang together. "Ta Ra

Ra Boom De Ay!"

After fifteen minutes of this they decided they should stop and get on with the search. They could, after all, dance as much as they wanted after they had made the Discovery. Somewhere in this dark and beckoning hall was the final resting place of their Pharaoh. It was up to them to find it.

They gathered all the tools and, fully laden, moved amidst the forest of columns. Jim tore up small scraps of notepaper as they went, and in this way they left a trail so they would be able to retrace their steps through the maze.

The columns went on and on. Whenever Jim and Doris reached what they thought would be the last row, the light would melt away the gloom and they would be confronted by yet another series.

Doris read the hieroglyphs at random, but no clues were revealed. Most of them told of battles fought and won in Upper and Lower Egypt by Martenarten, or of the healing powers of Ta, or of the activities of the Pharaoh's family. There were no directions to a burial chamber.

Eventually they came to a high wall and the columns stopped. At the base of the wall, set into the alabaster floor, was a round well filled with dark water.

"Doris, look! A holy well. It must come from the Nile."

"But that's kilometres away."

"Where there's a well, there's a way—"

"To what?"

"To the Holy of Holies."

He took the lamp from her and held it high to light up the length of the wall.

A few metres down to the right, they saw a darker recess. Together they crept to it, their footsteps light, as though they were walking on air. Jim shone the lamp into the small square room slightly below them.

"Raaaark!" squealed Doris.

A small animal's face glared into their light. The animal's head and shoulders were covered with the stiff headdress of a Pharaoh.

"It's all right, my dear," said Jim. "It's only the guardian of the altar boat."

As they descended the three steps leading into the room, they saw the boat of the altar resting on a tall block of anthracite, just as it had been placed thousands of years earlier. It was a metre long and supported on poles twice that length; it was slightly over a metre high and the dusty cedar wood was carved in the finest detail.

"That animal gave me the squawks," said Doris, regaining her composure.

Jim laughed. "There's nothing to fear, not now."

He placed the tools in a corner while Doris took the torch and scanned the hieroglyph-covered walls.

After some minutes she called to Jim.

"What, my dear?" he answered.

"Can I have a brush?"

He rummaged through the knapsack until he found one.

"This could be of some interest," she said, taking the brush and sweeping the dust from a patch of carvings.

"What do they say?" Jim asked. He saw only a mass of legs, wings, human figures, moons, eyes and other assorted ancient shapes.

"Let's see." She cleared her throat, which had become scratchy from the dust. Then she read slowly:

They who can fly,
they who can write,
they with four legs,
they who possess these likenesses,
they will be ready.
They will conquer the darkness of this sepulchre
and find the side of light.

"Of course!" Jim gasped. "Of course! Why didn't I remember it before? The Riddle of Ta."

"The Riddle of Ta?"

"The famous Riddle of Ta. Every archaeologist worth his or her salt knows of it. It's carved into the Rosetta Stone!"

"Oh?"

"When they found the Rosetta, they didn't know why the Riddle was included. No one knew where the Riddle had come from because no one knew where the tomb was. How it appeared there is a mystery." Jim ran his fingers over the carvings. "Perhaps the last High Priest who left this tomb alive added it to the Stone." He looked at his friend.

"And we've got the real McCoy," she said.

"Doris!"

"Raark!" she jumped.

"Read it again."

"Again?"

"Slowly."

She moved the torch across the carvings and began to read. "They who can fly—"

"That's you," said Jim. "You can fly."

"—they who can write—"

"Me. That's me and my poems."

"—they with four legs—"

"Four legs?" wondered Jim. "Four legs? I wonder what—"

"I've got two," Doris chirped.

"And so have I," said Jim.

"Put them together and we've got—"

"Four! We—'they'—have four!"

Doris continued. "They who possess these likenesses, they will be ready. They will conquer the darkness of this sepulchre and find the side of light."

Jim clapped his hands together. "That's it, Doris, That's it! We're here, we possess the qualities described in this prophecy, we are poised, ready, we've overcome the traps and the cobwebs, we are 'they'. The side of light is ours!"

Then he stopped.

"There's only one problem," he said slowly.

"What's that?"

"How do we get there?"

"Search me," said the macaw.

"There must be something in here—some kind of guiding arrow." He padded around the walls, his fingers seeking some kind of lever or trigger or something to show them the way.

"Hang on," Doris said, "here's something else. Underneath the Riddle." She fetched the brush and had another dust.

"What is it?" Jim asked from the other side of the altar boat.

She read silently, then clucked.

"What, Doris?"

"Wouldn't you know it? A poem."

"Decipher it. It might guide us."

Doris shrugged. "Why not?" She read it through again, then recited in a sing-song voice:

The beak of a bird
will bring forth the light
to dispel the gloom
and make nothingness bright.

When she had finished, she threw up her wings. "What did I tell you?" she flarped. "This place only seems to be full of riddles and poems and cobwebs and booby traps.

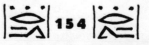

154

I reckon that's all we'll find. More of the same. I bet there's no treasure at all. Reerark!"

In exasperation she whacked the full-stop at the end of the inscription with her beak.

And the remarkable happened: there was a shudder, and the altar boat slid down into the floor with a gravelly crunch.

Jim and Doris looked at each other as it disappeared. Without a word, they gathered the tools and, with lamp and torch blazing, descended into the brooding darkness of the newly found pit.

Sixteen steps, hewn into the limestone, led them down in a steep curve. The steps were narrow and slippery and the pair had to be careful not to lose their footing. They moved warily but firmly and were soon near the bottom.

There, Doris's light bobbed over some white objects strewn across the last few steps.

"*Raaaaaaaaaaaaaaaaaarrrrrrrrrkkkk!*" she screamed, the sound rocketing up the stairwell.

"Don't be afraid, Doris," whispered Jim, lighting up the two ancient skeletons lying ahead of them. "They won't hurt you."

"Let's get past quickly," she squawked.

"They're probably the last of the slaves who knew of this secret passageway," Jim said as they stepped carefully over the crumbling piles of bones. "The guards would have killed them to make sure the secret stayed safe."

"Not the sort of job you'd want to get up in the morning for," thought the macaw as she hopped across a brittle ribcage. "Why, I'd rather be a poodle than a slave, especially if being a slave meant ending up— *Oooh!*"

Everywhere brighter than the sun.

Before them lay a huge, narrow chamber with gold-painted walls, silver-mooned ceiling, and thousands of pieces of ancient treasure.

Down the centre of the chamber, set into the ground, lay a canal of sparkling water, still and tranquil. The canal floor was inlaid with precious emeralds and diamonds. These, together with the glint of gold from the treasure-lined walls, cast off such a reflection from Jim's and Doris's lights that the whole place was lit more radiantly than anything they had ever seen.

They found their pairs of desert sun-spectacles and put them over their dazzled eyes. Now the glare was less harsh and they were able to see everything in clear detail. Their flabbergastedness increased as they beheld the priceless collection.

Closest to them, a gigantic pair of statues of Pharaoh Martenarten stood majestically, their outstretched hands holding gold crescent moons.

"Look at that fine nose," gasped Jim. "That strong jaw, those powerful eyes. His commanding dimples. The face of a King if ever I saw one."

Doris whistled in agreement and waddled off between the legs of one of the Martenartens. Away she

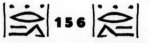

went along the left side of the chamber, her beak open in awe. Jim jumped across the canal and began to make his way down the right side, inspecting the amazing hoard. Every so often they would shout across the gleaming water and tell each other of an especially exciting item.

There were beds of pure gold and silver, all lined up neatly one next to the other, their bases woven from the finest spun gold. These had been placed for the King's rest before his spirit left the Tomb to go forth into the After Life. Nearby, a high broad shelf was filled with hundreds of wooden statues of different sizes, all finely carved and gilded, and every one of them was Martenarten.

Circular plates of silver and gold rested on top of large ivory boxes inlaid with panels of coloured glass. Doris peered through the panels in one of these and blinked at the sparkle from the jumble of bracelets, rings and amulets crammed inside.

Jim lifted the lid of an ebony box and found it to be chock full of diamond and ruby necklaces. Nearby, six diadems of canary-yellow gold and red carnelian were stacked carelessly, as though someone had dropped them in a hurry. They rested against a painted wooden screen showing the King in his chariot hunting ostrich, gazelle, deer and lions.

Doris came across two thrones of carved wood, encased in gold and richly ornamented with semiprecious stones, glass and silver. Their arms were in the shape of two crowned serpents with long, many-feathered wings, and on their back panels a large image of Ta was embossed, with silver moon-rays extending in shimmering lines.

Alabaster boxes with knobs of obsidian; bronze scimitars; headrests of turquoise-blue glass and carved ivory; alabaster vases of breathtaking white frostiness; pottery wine jars and perfume bottles; small model boats of painted wood; a bronze sceptre in the shape of a crook, covered with gold and glass; lapis lazuli amulets; boomerangs and throw-sticks; all these things they stumbled upon, as eager as children under a Christmas tree on Christmas morning. Each discovery proved to be more astonishing than the last and the pair were once again invaded by marauding squadrons of goosebumps.

Jim stopped by a gold vulture, three metres high. "Look, Doris," he called. "It could've been your mother."

"Ha, ha," said Doris. She flew across the canal and came to perch on the beak of the statue. Her torch lit up the enormous garnet eyes, making them fiery and incandescent.

"And look at this," Jim gasped, pointing to the massive chariot parked next to it. He ran his hands over the heavy spokes of the wheel, up and over the curve of the hub. "I wonder how many times the King rode in this?"

Next to the chariot were three large couches placed

end to end and supported by fantastic carved animals with slender bodies and lions' paws. The heads of the animals were unusual, a cross between the hippopotamus and the crocodile, with ivory teeth and red-stained tongues.

"Probably to keep evil spirits away from the Pharaoh," Jim explained.

Many objects were piled on and below the couches: gold pectorals in the forms of human-headed birds with wings of midnight-blue glass; large lapis lazuli scarabs; more gold bracelets with the "mystic eye" set into them in red glass, amethyst and malachite; silver daggers; a couple of splendorous maces of gilded wood; ceremonial walking sticks and staffs; a small black-varnished shrine featuring a bright crescent moon; military trumpets of silver; long-handled ostrich-feathered fans as perfect as if they had been made yesterday; tools of wood and bronze; and many handsome boxes.

Jim carefully moved an alabaster chalice from the top of one of the boxes. He took his pocket-knife and, holding his breath, prised open the box's lid. It came easily. This box was filled with clothes of the Pharaoh – belts, sandals of leather and gold, gloves, richly decorated bolts of fabric, wigs. Everything was as if it were new, untouched by time.

Doris popped onto his shoulder and cooed as he turned over piece after piece.

After a while, he closed the lid and stood. He looked at the far end of the chamber and began walking

purposefully towards it, past the array of delicate translucent alabaster lamps which littered the floor, striding over the papyrus hampers and the ebony statuettes on their golden pedestals, until he came to a line of four small jars. They were pure white and on their lids a realistic likeness of the King's head had been carved. These were the canopic jars in which the King's internal organs had been preserved.

"There it is, my dear," he whispered, and every fibre in his body tingled. "There it is."

Beyond the canopic jars lay the mighty sarcophagus of Pharaoh Martenarten.

With scarcely beating hearts, they made their way to the burial platform. Jim pulled out his matches and lit two small torches hanging at an angle from the rear wall. They flickered to life, illuminating the heavy casket, making the thick gold shine until it became a sea of dazzling yellow bobbing with jewels.

Jim and Doris were speechless. Never in their wildest dreams had they imagined such a colossal, glittering vision.

This was the outer casket. There would be, as was typical of a Pharaoh's state, two more caskets inside this, each one smaller than the last, each one brighter and more jewelled. In the third casket the King would be lying.

They mounted the platform and stood close to this wonderful thing. Cairo Jim ran his hands gently along the top, over the sculptured gold hands of the Pharaoh,

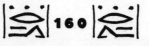

clasped and holding the long striped sceptre and the knotted flail. He blew the talc-dust from the face. He was beside himself with goosebumps, so much so that even his eyebrows prickled.

"The time for dreaming has finished," he whispered. "Our months of searching are at an end."

Doris stared at the carved golden head with its blue-striped headdress. Instead of eyes, she saw big pools of blackness gazing up at the cobwebbed, moon-filled ceiling. With her wing she caressed the commanding dimples near the King's mouth.

She turned to Jim. "How can this sarcophagus be a thing of death when it's so full of life?"

Jim smiled. "The magic of the ancient casket painters," he said quietly. "Grand masters of their trade." He took his pocket-knife and started to run it between the lid and the base.

"Jim?"

"What, my dear?"

"It's all so beautiful."

"It certainly is."

"And it's all been here for so very long."

"It certainly has."

"Why do we have to disturb it then?"

Jim stopped running the knife along the lid. "What do you mean, my dear?"

"Well, can't we just leave it? Does it *have* to go to the Cairo Museum? Why can't it all just stay here?"

"Discovery is one thing, Doris, knowledge another.

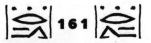

Only when all this magnificence is in the Museum will it be safe from unscrupulous tomb robbers. And there's a good chance we'll be able to learn things we wouldn't have otherwise known."

"Such as?"

"We could discover more about our ancient ancestors, and," he dropped his voice to a whisper, for what he was thinking was truly astonishing, "we could discover more about ourselves…"

"Cooo," coooed Doris.

"Just think, my dear," he said, dislodging a thick layer of dust and sand, "just think what's in here. The mummy of this mysterious King lies wrapped and waiting for us alone—"

"That's what you think, you poetic archaeologist, you," a voice snarled from the other end of the canal.

Jim dropped the knife as he and Doris jumped in alarm. Their eyes shot to the base of the skeleton-strewn stairs.

There stood Captain Neptune Bone, the flea-ridden Desdemona perched menacingly on his shoulder with a lighted candle strapped to the top of her head.

Bone wore his deep vermilion fez and was aiming an antique blunderbuss musket directly at them. Doris screeched loudly into the chamber, a long, drawn-out scream, but the sound only rose to the musty ceiling where it was quickly swallowed up by the ancient cobwebs.

▲▲▲▲▲ **10** ▲▲▲▲▲

THWARTED BY A BLUNDERBUSS

BLACK SUNLIGHT.

Cairo Jim blinked as he emerged from the dimness of the first gallery and into the pit Brenda had accidentally unearthed. With a grunt, Neptune Bone squirmed after him, through the hole in the cedar Door. (By no means an easy feat – it was a tight and sweaty squeeze.) The light streaming down the shaft stung Jim's eyes with its sudden glare and he went to reach into his shirt pocket for his sun-spectacles, having removed them after leaving the chamber of Martenarten.

Bone rammed the blunderbuss hard into his back. "Hands clear, Jim," he snarled. "Keep 'em in the air. Arrr, that's the way. I don't want to fire just yet."

"What are you doing here, Bone?" Jim asked, the perspiration building on his brow.

"Following you, my old friend. Not a hard thing to do, by any means. So considerate of you to leave your little trail along the way." He let several pieces of the torn-up notepaper flutter from his hand. "It was a great help to Desdemona and myself."

"Ouch!" shrieked Doris as Desdemona jabbed and pushed her through the hole in the Door. "Mind the plumage!"

"Don't worry, technicolour talons," throbbed the raven, "I'll be doing that sooner than you imagine." And she let out a fiendish cackle.

"What's your game, then?" Jim asked Bone. "Why the blunderbuss?"

"I'll explain everything when we get to the top."

"And how will we do that? There's no rope."

"That's what you think." Bone looked skyward and cupped his mouth with his free hand. "Rhampsinites twins," he called. "Throw down the rope!"

"I might have known," said Jim in disgust.

Suddenly a blurred object whizzed towards them on the end of a rope. They all pressed themselves close against the walls of the shaft as the object hurtled to the ground, landing with a thud. "Ouch," moaned the object.

"Abdullah, you idiot—" began Bone.

"I am Kelvin – ooh, my head—"

"Kelvin, you idiot, when I told you to tie a weight to the end, I meant something substantially smaller."

"Yes, Captain Bone."

Abdullah's head popped over the top of the hole. "Do you want to come up now?" he grinned toothlessly.

"No, Abdullah, we'd prefer to dance," Bone said, rolling his eyes.

"But there's not all that much room—"

"*Of course we want to come up, you nincompoop!*"

"Why, thank you, Captain Bone. Okay, I'll hold this end. Come up when you like." His head retreated quickly.

Bone turned to Jim and Doris. "I'll go first, but don't get any smart ideas about escaping," he threatened. He stroked the blunderbuss with his delicate pudgy fingers. "Remember, I have the power."

As Jim watched him haul and swivel his way up the rope, he began to weigh up the situation. Whatever Bone was up to, he thought, it was no good. There was no way he and Doris could make any attempt to escape from down here – the only place to go was back into the ground, and that would only put them back where they are now. Bone had been clever to go up the rope first; it meant he was always in a position to keep his gun aimed at them. And what of Brenda? Where was she?

Doris struggled in the clutches of Desdemona, trying to break free.

"No, Doris," Jim said calmly. "Don't fight. It'll only make things worse."

The macaw looked at him, her eyes clouded and worried. "Whatever you say," she spluttered.

The fez appeared above, followed by Bone's face and the wide bore of the weapon. "Arr. Up you come, Jim. And no quick moves, d'you hear? I have a very anxious trigger finger. Desdemona!"

"What, my Captain?"

"Stop scratching and fly up with the feathers."

"How rude," said Doris.

"Shut your beak and come with me." The raven planted her jaws around Doris's tailfeathers and soared

up and out of the hole.

"Yaaaaawwww," screeched Doris, battling with her wings.

"I'll get you for this, Bone," Jim seethed, inching his way up the rope.

"Oh, you will, will you?"

"You bet your blunderbuss."

Kelvin sat on the ground, rubbing his head and his backside in turn. "But Captain Bone, what about me?" he yelled. "How will I get up?"

"You can stay," answered Bone. "It'll be safer with you out of the way."

Kelvin frowned and rubbed his eyepatch. "Ooohh," he whined.

When Jim arrived at the top a terrible sight greeted him: Brenda the Wonder Camel lying on the ground, bound, gagged and trussed.

"Brenda, my lovely," he cried, rushing to her. She gave a muffled snort through her gag and looked at him with big, sad eyes.

"That's far enough, Cairo Jim!" Bone pointed the gun and Jim stopped in his tracks.

"What have you done, you villain?" Jim was furious.

"She's unharmed, don't you fear. Being a stupid, dumb beast, she won't be able to tell anyone what's going on here this afternoon, will she? So there's no real sense in getting rid of her. A waste of ammunition really. We've just bundled her up a little bit so she won't make a nuisance of herself."

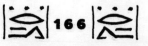

"She's not stupid," Doris objected loudly. "She's a Wonder Camel!"

Desdemona poked Doris sharply. "Can I have her now?" she asked Bone, her eyes becoming redder and redder.

"Soon enough," Bone smirked. He sat on a large rock, still aiming his weapon at Jim and Doris, and lit a cigar.

"Medical authorities warn that smoking is a health hazard," Jim said.

"So are blunderbusses," growled Bone. "Tie him, Kelvin."

"Abdullah," said Abdullah.

"Tie him anyway."

Abdullah sniggered and took out a bundle of ancient bandages, which he started to wind raggedly around Jim's body.

"What the—?"

"I'll tell you 'what the—?'," Bone leered. "I'll tell you all. You see, Cairo Jim, I'm here this afternoon because I want something."

"What do you want:"

"I want Martenarten."

"You what?"

"I want your Pharaoh."

Jim gritted his teeth. "No way," he almost spat. "There's no way you or anyone else will get what's down there. It's going straight to the Cairo Museum after it's all been thoroughly catalogued!"

"Oh, that'll happen," Bone said matter-of-factly, his

fez tassel blowing in the wind. "It'll be thoroughly catalogued. Although not all of it, perhaps. Maybe a few pieces will accidentally fall onto the back of a truck, if you know what I mean—"

"I know exactly what you mean, you underhanded archaeologist."

"—and the rest will, quite rightly, be deposited with the Museum in Cairo." He puffed on his cigar. "What I meant when I said I want Martenarten is: I want to be the one who *discovered* him."

"But you didn't," Doris squawked. "Jim did."

"And you and Brenda too, Doris," pointed out Jim.

"Arrr, yes," Bone sighed. "That's the bother of it all. Which is why I'm here now, you see. To rewrite history"

"How do you think you'll do that?" Jim asked angrily.

Bone held the blunderbuss high. "What do you think I've got loaded into this?" he asked.

"Let me see," Doris said. "Good manners? Charm? Perhaps some dietary pills? If it's any of the above, why don't you turn the gun on yourself?"

Bone's eyes flashed at her, his pupils seemingly about to burst. Then he took a long drag on the tobacco and relaxed. "Very droll, Dorothy," he said, blowing smoke at her.

"The name's Doris. Doris Salaam."

"I'm sorry. I had a friend named Dorothy once. No, what I've got in my weapon is something I'm sure you'll be familiar with, Jim."

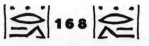

"What?"

"You've heard of 'elephant gel', I presume? Having spent time in the Emnobellian jungles, you've seen it used?"

Cairo Jim went pale. He had seen the elephant doctors use it to drug the giant creatures prior to ingrown-toenail operations. It was a powerful, slimy drug which upon contact with the skin could put any other living creature to sleep for up to six months. He nodded in dread.

"I thought you'd know it," Bone continued. "What I plan for you is something quite unique. A quick squirt of this, a careful bandaging job, and you're going to become a mummy. We'll send you up to Cairo with the rest of the treasures. I'll tell them you were Martenarten's pal or something, and we found you in a casket near the King's. I'll even make sure they put you in a special display case, high above the other exhibits. It's what you've always wanted, after all: a tomb with a view."

Desdemona laughed loudly. "Nevermore, nevermore, nevermore. Ha ha ha ha ha!"

"And then," said Bone, flicking his ash, "Bob's your uncle."

"That's right," came Kelvin's whine from the pit, "but leave him out of this."

"You'll never get away with it!" Jim shouted.

"Oh, no?" puffed Bone.

"No," replied Jim confidently. "There's one thing you haven't taken into account."

"And what's that?" sneered the fez-wearing man.

"The Riddle of Ta."

Bone cast a sideways smirk at Desdemona. Then he threw back his head and laughed loudly.

"What's so funny?" asked Doris.

He stopped his cacophonous bellowing and addressed her. "The Riddle of Ta?" he said haughtily. "The Riddle of Ta? Arrr."

"It's in the Holy of Holies," Jim said. "We found it on our way to the burial chamber. It told us we have the necessary qualities to—"

With one swift movement, Bone aimed his blunderbuss at the head of Cairo Jim. "I was talking to the bird," he snarled. "Have the courtesy not to interrupt." He kept the gun aimed at Jim but fixed his eye once again on Doris. "Tell me, oh gaudy Dolly—"

"Doris!"

"Tell me of this Riddle. I *have* read it, once upon a time, but I remember it only vaguely. Kindly refresh my memory."

Doris struggled as Desdemona dug her claws into the macaw's wings.

"Go on, sing," the raven croaked. "He doesn't like to be kept waiting."

"It's carved into the wall, near where the altar boat was," Doris said against her will.

"And what," Bone asked as though she were a stupid creature, "what pray tell does this Riddle say?"

"Tell him, Doris," urged Jim. "Make him see he's got no claim."

The yellow-and-blue macaw looked Bone in the eye. She puffed out her chest feathers, and taking a deep breath, recited the Riddle.

When she had finished, Jim said, "Don't you see, you treacherous man? All those things point to us. *We* possess those likenesses!"

At this, Bone burst into laughter. His belly wobbled under the emerald-green waistcoat and his cheeks quivered and turned red beneath his bristly beard. When his mirth subsided, he puffed on his cigar and looked vastly superior. His eyes flashed like a dragon's.

"*You*?" he questioned. "You think so, eh, poet? We'll see about that." He reached into the back pocket of his plus-fours and withdrew a flat bundle. In the hazy light it appeared to be a bundle of papers, but Cairo Jim couldn't be sure.

"Now, let's see," he mumbled, balancing them on his knee. "How did that Riddle go again?" He cleared his throat loudly and threw the cigar to the ground. "Arrr. Like this, I think: 'They who can fly' … why, upon my soul, Buzz Aldrin could fly, couldn't he? He flew all the way to the moon." From the bundle, he held up the black-and-white photograph of the astronaut.

"'They who can write'," he continued. "Here's two fine writers." He held up Edith Sitwell and Alice B. Toklas.

"'They with four legs'." Out came Rin Tin Tin.

"'They will be ready'." He picked out the rubbing of Ethelred the Unready and, holding one end of it in his mouth and juggling the blunderbuss, tore it fiercely in half.

"'They will conquer' – Will Conquer." Out came that particular lithograph.

"'The darkness of this sepulchre and find the side of light.'"

"Where did you get those?" Jim shouted. "They were in my tent. They're mine!"

"Arrr, no they're not. They're *mine*. Always have been. For ever and a day. You see, you're not the only one who's read the Rosetta Stone. Oh, yeeesss," he said suddenly, as though an electric light bulb had flashed over his head, "there was one line I forgot, wasn't there? What was it? Ah, I remember: 'They who possess these likenesses.' That's it."

He threw the collection of likenesses at Jim's feet. "So there you have it," Bone said smugly. "*I* am 'they'. I have the right to Pharaoh Martenarten."

Jim flexed his muscles against his bindings, trying to break through them. "You're deranged, Bone," he shouted. "It's all poppycock! You have no right. You're a madman!"

Suddenly Bone stood and lifted the blunderbuss to his shoulder, aiming it at Jim's head. "That's enough of your chat," he growled. "Desdemona! The time has come. Take your prize and do your worst."

"Oh, thank you, thank you, thank you," the raven drooled, her yellow tongue hanging out. She threw a hessian bag over Doris's head and upturned the bewildered macaw.

"Raaaark!"

"What's happening?" cried Jim. "What's she going to do with her?"

"Shut up," said Bone.

"Captain, are you going to come and watch?"

"No," Bone said, screwing up his nose. "I hate the sight of quills."

"Suit yourself," said the raven. She grasped the bag in her claws and took off into the sky. "See you back at camp. Ha ha ha ha ha!"

Abdullah watched them growing smaller and smaller, glad that the feathered threats had at last gone.

"Bone, you've gone too far!" Jim shouted, struggling against the bandages.

"No, Cairo Jim, I'm about to do that now."

Bone squinted as he lined up an imaginary dot dead in the centre of Jim's eyebrows. In another second, the vile yellow gel would spurt out in an unstoppable jet, and history would be his oyster.

"If I were a more decent man, I'd offer you a last shergold," he taunted mercilessly. "But them's the breaks. Arrr. Bye bye, Jim. Pleasant dreams."

Jim shut his eyes as he heard Brenda snort wildly. Captain Neptune Bone took his final aim, smiling as his finger curled around the trigger. He chuckled deep down inside and his beard bristled.

There was an almighty *clunk*, and he lowered the gun to his side.

▲▲▲▲▲ **11** ▲▲▲▲▲

THE LUGGAGE OF THE VALKYRIE

ABDULLAH Rhampsinites fell backwards with a shocked grunt, beaned by a set of golf clubs which had fallen from the sky.

Jim opened his eyes and saw Abdullah's unconscious figure splayed under the weight.

"Merciful heavens!" gasped Bone, horrified. Shielding his eyes from the sun, he looked up. A large bag of croquet mallets was heading towards them, hurtling down at great speed. "What the—?"

He dived out of the way as the mallets disappeared into the pit. There was silence, then a whining scream from Kelvin, then another, louder *clunk*.

"Abdullah?" called Bone.

"It was Kelvin," said Jim.

"Kelvin?"

But there was no answer.

Without warning, an orange hula-hoop landed very close to Brenda, and Jim's heart soared. "They who can fly," he said quietly.

Out of the wild blue yonder, a parachuted figure glided down and landed between Jim and Bone. It was clearly a woman and, as the silken canopy billowed and draped along the sand, Jim noticed that she was wearing

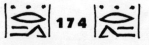

special-issue Valkyrian Airways parachuting jodhpurs.

She took off her goggles and leather helmet and shook out her curly auburn hair.

"Oh, Jocelyn, Jocelyn Osgood," Jim's heart pounded.

"Jim, great news!" she said in her cool and confident voice (an excellent thing in a woman, Jim had always thought). "There's a catering strike with Valkyrian, so no passenger services. I thought I'd visit—" She saw the yellowing bandages around his arms and legs. "Oh, am I interrupting something?"

"You certainly are," Bone snarled..

She turned and laid eyes on him for the first time in many years. "Why, if it isn't Neptune Bone."

"Jocelyn Osgood," breathed Bone, his heart turning even more sour.

"What's going on?" she asked, eyeing the blunderbuss.

"Jocelyn, he's trying to claim Martenarten!" Jim blurted.

"You've found him?" cried Jocelyn, unstrapping herself from her harness. "Oh, Jim, congratulations!"

Bone raised the gun. "That's enough out of you, Cairo Jim," he warned. He thought quickly. "Jocelyn, there's no reason for you to be involved in all this."

"But, Neptune, you know that whatever involves Jim also involves me."

"That needn't be the case. I'll make a deal with you: if you promise to turn your head, and then to spend regular intervals of your life with me, I'll make sure you

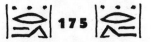

have all the gold you've ever wanted."

Jocelyn Osgood stared at the crazed Captain. "Well, of all the nerve," she scoffed. Hands on her hips, she laughed defiantly into his face.

The sound of her laughter was too much for Bone. "Right, right, *right*!" he screamed. "Have it your own way. Only don't say I didn't warn you. Your turn's next!" He aimed the gun once again at Cairo Jim's head. "People. Bah!"

Bone did not hear the drone of Jocelyn's travelling trunk until it was too late. Looking up, he saw the huge square shadow of it almost on top of him. He dropped the gun and threw up his precious manicured hands in a feeble attempt to protect himself, but it was no use.

There was the biggest *clunk* of all, and Neptune Bone was instantly pile-driven into the soft sand. He disappeared with a whimper.

"Ah, I was wondering where that'd got to," Jocelyn beamed as she rushed to unwrap Jim.

"Jocelyn, your timing has always been impeccable," he smiled.

For a brief moment their eyes met, hers wide and clear, his warm and grateful. Then the bandages fell away and he quickly put on his desert sun-spectacles.

"Come on," he said urgently, taking her by the arm. "We must untie Brenda and get to Doris. There's not a moment to waste while she's in the clutches of that diabolical raven!"

"Roger," she said.

"Leave Cousin out of this," came a stunned voice from the pit.

They raced to the Wonder Camel, who lay snorting and squirming in the sand. Jocelyn ripped the gag from her mouth while Jim unravelled the bindings Abdullah (or was it Kelvin?) had fashioned.

"Quuuaaaaaooo."

Jocelyn busied herself with the saddle.

She licked Jim's hands and face (Brenda, not Jocelyn) and fluttered her eyelashes with great relief. As he felt her pointy tongue sliding over his cheeks, he realised he hadn't shaved for several days, and hoped Jocelyn wouldn't mind his appearance too much.

"Okay," said Jocelyn, strapping the saddle over Brenda's humps, "Let's make tracks!"

They got on and Brenda sprang up, her legs like elastic.

"Do you know the way?" Jim asked her.

She snorted. "I'll find her, don't worry," she nodded. "I'm not a Wonder Camel for nothing."

Jim swung her around and, with her nostrils flaring, she thundered towards the Valley of the Queens.

"Raaaaaaaarrrk!" screeched Doris, struggling under the weight of the rocks that pinioned her wings to the ground. "Let me go, you fleabag!"

Desdemona hopped about her in a circle, her eyes throbbing with glee. "Ha ha ha," she cackled. "I'll let you go when I've had my way."

"And what's that, you grotesque guckbucket?"

The raven stopped hopping and bent over her. "Sticks and stones may break my bones," she gloated, "but at least I'll go out fully feathered."

Doris frowned. "Eh?" she squawked.

"You have no idea what it's like to be *drab*, have you? You've never had people look at you as though you're the shabbiest of shabbies. When was the last time a rat scampered away because he found the sight of you disgusting? Never, I'll bet. Because you're so colourful and bright. Everyone has time for *you*."

"Beauty comes from the inside," said Doris. "it doesn't matter what you *look* like."

"Rubbish," Desdemona croaked, pecking a flea from her belly.

"What's important is who you are."

"And clothes maketh the man, or in this case, the bird. Which is why I've got you, here, now." She bent very close, her seaweed breath wafting into Doris's face. "I'm going to pluck every feather from your body," she said slowly. "One by one, until you're nothing but a prickled pile of pink flesh. Then I'm going to make a cloak with them, one with a little sash to go round my neck. And then when I fly past, everyone will say, "There goes Desdemona, that most splendiferous of ravens". And I'll get prompt service in restaurants and no one'll step on me in the dark!"

Doris shut her eyes and wailed loudly.

"It's no use, macaw," Desdemona laughed. "Out

here, no one can hear you squawk." She straightened up and pinched a feather on Doris's head. "Soon your beauty will be nevermore."

"Let go! Reeerraaark! Don't touch me!"

She pinched the feather tighter and was about to pull it, when the air went strangely still.

"What's that doing there?" asked the raven, looking up. A big mauve cosmetic case with the initials "J.O." on it was plummeting quickly down.

"*Aaaaaaaarrrrk!*" she howled, letting go of Doris's plume and stepping back.

The case *clunked* on her skull, flattening her to the ground and knocking her completely out.

There was a thunder of camel-hoofs, and then Jim's voice: "Doris! My dearest, are you all right?"

She managed to move her head until she could see them. "Croak the raven nevermore," she prerked happily.

Jim leapt off and rushed to her. He threw the rocks from her wings and helped her up.

"A little bruised," she said, inspecting herself, "but otherwise none the worse for wear." She hopped onto his shoulder and nuzzled against his neck. "So, he didn't gel you?"

"No," he said, stroking her beak. "And, Brenda, you're okay?"

The Wonder Camel grinned and snorted. "We're all okay, thanks to Miss Osgood."

"Hello, Doris, my darling," said Jocelyn, opening up

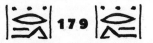

the cosmetic case and taking out a long, spotted ribbon.

"Raaaaark!" screamed Doris.

"I've got something for you. Come here."

Doris looked at the ribbon, then at Jim.

"Go on," he whispered. "You deserve it."

She fluttered over and nestled on her arm. Jocelyn tied the ribbon gently around the bird's head feathers.

"There," she said as she straightened it. "Doesn't she look grand?"

And, not being able to help herself, Doris's beak flapped up into her face with a loud *thwaaaaaaanggg*, much to the amusement of Cairo Jim.

◬◬◬◬◬ **12** ◬◬◬◬◬

BRIGHTER THAN THE SUN

SIX MONTHS LATER, when all the artefacts had been boxed and catalogued and brought to Cairo, a special opening ceremony was held in the magnificent Museum.

Miss Pyrella Frith, looking splendid in a new white lace dress, was busily running around straightening the enormous photographs which hung from the walls. Jim had been true to his word and had engaged her as the official excavation photographer. She had worked hard and tirelessly alongside Jim, Doris and Brenda, and the wonderful pictures she had taken reflected her efforts.

Everybody was present, all of them bubbling with excitement. In one corner of the entrance hall, Mrs Amun-Ra was engaged in conversation with Gerald Perry Esquire. Since the publicity surrounding the Discovery, his pigeon restaurants had taken off and had become extremely profitable, and he had found no trouble in financing the rest of the excavation. Now he stood blinking in the brightness of the entrance hall, a very wealthy man, still wearing the same white suit.

"Well," said Mrs Amun-Ra in her big floral frock and her new hat piled almost to the ceiling with

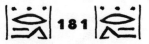

181

artificial vegetables, "I bet you are an excitable man today, are you not, Mr Perry Esquire?"

"Mmm? Oh, yes," said Gerald Perry. "Very. I hardly slept a wink last night."

"I am not surpassed," she said, adjusting her hat under all the weight. "It is a very hysterical occasion. The first-ever exhibition of Pharaoh Martenarten. Oh, my goodness me. So marvellous for Mr Jim and Miss Doris and Miss Brenda, is it not?"

"Absolutely, Mrs Amun-Ra. Absolutely."

"Of course, me I always knew they would do it. It was written by the stars, you know. My friends are a credit to Egypt."

Suddenly she spied someone on the other side of the crowd. "Oh, Mr Perry Esquire," she said, smoothing down her frock, "will you excuse me? I've just seen someone I know."

"Of course."

"Ah, Buzz!" she cried, making her way through the throng. "What do you think of my rhubarbs, then?"

Gerald Perry looked at his watch. "Hmm," he thought. "It's nearly time for Jim to make his speech. I wonder where they are?"

There was a small flurry as several newspaper reporters and photographers scampered to the entrance. The crowd of Old Relics Society members shuffled out of the way as Cairo Jim and Doris rode into the entrance hall on Brenda the Wonder Camel, who was resplendent with her new, colourful macramé saddle.

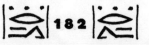

"It's Cairo Jim," shouted Esmond Horneplush.

"Bravo!" everyone cheered. Camera flashbulbs burst as photographers tried to get a good angle.

Gerald Perry rushed to greet them. "Jim, you're late," he flustered. "Everyone's waiting for your speech."

"Have you seen Miss Osgood?" Jim asked, looking through the crowd.

"Hmm? No, can't say I have."

"Oh, dear, I wonder where she is. She said she'd be here."

"Never mind about that. Hello, Doris, Brenda."

"Raark."

"Quaao."

"Everyone's waiting—"

"All right, then." Jim, Brenda and Doris climbed the steps of the rostrum. Gerald Perry followed closely behind.

"Ladies, gentlemen and everyone else," said Perry, blowing into the microphone. "I would like to present to you the man, the macaw and the camel of the hour: Cairo Jim and his colleagues!"

A sea of applause swelled from the gathering. Gerald Perry stepped aside and Jim dismounted and took the microphone. As he was about to begin his speech, he glimpsed a familiar figure arriving at the back. He smiled as she removed her goggles and flying helmet.

She returned his smile, her pearly teeth flashing. She gave him a thumbs-up sign, and he began:

You've gathered here today to see
antiquities astounding,
great treasures which left us all three
astonished at their founding.

The road to this discovery
was not without its bumps,
thanks to a rascal dastardly,
but, sure as Brenda's humps,

We persevered, we did not run,
despite his evil ways,
and now we're brighter than the sun
on this, the best of days.

So Doris, Brenda and myself
will now present the treasure
which we rescued from pit and shelf
and catalogued with pleasure.

We've brought it up to old Cairo
in crate and box and carton ...
and thus, my friends, 'tis time to show
the gold of Martenarten!

Everybody decided then that Cairo Jim was a very fine
archaeologist.

They applauded again, so loudly this time that Mrs
Amun-Ra's vegetables wobbled. Then Gerald Perry

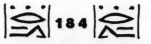

handed Jim a pair of golden scissors, and he and Doris cut through the ribbon that led into the Museum.

Amidst cheering and stomping, the throng moved towards the priceless treasures.

Gerald Perry took Jim by the arm and led him and Doris to one side. "Tell me, Jim," he said. "There's something I need to know. What became of Bone and his accomplices?"

Jim's eyes searched for Jocelyn over the mass of heads. "That we're not sure of," he said. "When we went back to the dig to retrieve Miss Osgood's luggage, he and the Rhampsinites twins were gone."

"And we didn't dare touch the raven for fear of getting fleas," Doris added.

"I wonder where they are," said Perry. "There are a few questions the Antiquity Police would like to ask them."

Jim turned to him. "Probably skulking in some darkened place," he answered. "Unfortunately, my dear Perry, naughtiness will always be lurking somewhere."

"I suppose you're right," Gerald Perry sighed.

"Hello there," said Jocelyn, appearing out of nowhere. "Mr Perry, would you mind if I borrowed these three for a little while?"

"Mmm? Oh, Miss Osgood, hello. No, not at all. Do, by all means."

She took Jim by the arm. "I'll have them back in a month."

"Eh? A month?"

"What's happening?" asked Jim.

"Come with me. You too, Brenda." She led them quickly out of the Museum and into the sunshine, where a specially adapted Sopwith aeroplane was waiting on the grass.

"I've chartered it," she told them. "The only time I get to do the flying myself. It's so tiresome being a Flight Attendant *all* the time – I *do* wish Valkyrian would let women pilots fly. That airline is appallingly old-fashioned."

"Coo," cooed Doris.

"Everyone in. Brenda, there's a special seat for you at the back. There should be enough room for your humps and saddle. There's a perch for you, Doris, in the middle. You'll find some of Mrs Amun-Ra's special shergolds in a bag under the seat."

"Is she in on this too?" asked Jim.

Jocelyn smiled and put on her helmet and goggles. "And you, my friend, can ride in the front with me."

"But—"

"Get in."

Jim knew it was no use arguing; Jocelyn Osgood could be a very determined woman. "We'd better do as she says, gang."

When they were all comfortably settled, Jocelyn pulled a knob and the wooden propeller spluttered to life, slicing through the air as it picked up speed. She reached down and jerked two ropes, releasing the wheel chocks.

The plane moved slowly towards the gates and out into the street, which had been closed by the authorities for this auspicious occasion and was totally free of traffic.

"Goodbye, Mr Jim," called Mrs Amun-Ra, coming out to see them off. She fluttered a pink osnaburg handkerchief above her radishes. "Come back soon, Miss Jocelyn. And you too, Miss Doris and Miss Brenda!"

"Bye, Jim," waved Pyrella Frith breathlessly. "Make sure you write, won't you?"

"Good work, Jim," Gerald Perry Esquire shouted. "Enjoy yourselves, wherever you're off to!"

Jim, Doris and Brenda all waved back as they hurtled down the main avenue towards Tahrir Street. Then Jocelyn pulled back on the joystick, and the aircraft lifted gently into the air.

They flew low over the city for some minutes, past the bazaars with their streets of galabiyya-makers and tent-weavers, out in a wide arc to the pyramids of the Giza plateau.

As they were approaching the Sphinx, Jim tapped his pilot on the shoulder of her flying jacket. "Tell me," he shouted above the noise of the propeller, "where exactly are we going?"

Jocelyn turned her goggled eyes to him. "You need a holiday," she shouted back. "You've all been working very hard."

"A holiday?" squawked Doris, her feathers blustering

in the wind. "Raaark! How about that, Brenda?"

The Wonder Camel snorted happily in the rear and shifted her humps against the leather seat. "Plenty of time to read," she thought.

"So I've arranged to take a few weeks off," Jocelyn continued.

Jim smiled. "That's all very good. But where are we going?"

She looked out into the clouds. "How does the Ivory Coast sound?" she asked.

"The Ivory Coast?" Jim's eyes lit up. "Really?" He leaned back and settled his head against the headrest. "It's certainly been an adventure," he thought. "A champion one at that."

The Sopwith climbed higher and higher, until it gradually became a mere speck against the mighty Egyptian sun.

The propeller thundered louder as they spiralled even higher. Then there was a sudden burst of speed and a puff of white smoke, and all at once the tiny speck disappeared into the thick blue blanket of the late afternoon sky.

THE END

Swoggle me sideways! Unearth more thrilling mysteries of history starring Cairo Jim, Doris, and Brenda the Wonder Camel – **THE CAIRO JIM CHRONICLES**

CAIRO JIM ON THE TRAIL TO CHACHA MUCHOS

Why did an ancient Peruvian tribe dance themselves to death? Can that well-known archaeologist and little-known poet Cairo Jim uncover the secrets of ChaCha Muchos before the evil Captain Bone? And will Jim *ever* get any poetry published… Find out in his first flabbergasting adventure!

CAIRO JIM AND THE SUNKEN SARCOPHAGUS OF SEKHERET

What sinister secrets lie hidden in the depths of the Red Sea? Will evil genius Captain Bone's greed for gold lead him to a watery grave? Has Cairo Jim's flabber finally been gasted? All will be revealed in his third flummoxing exploit!

CAIRO JIM AND THE ALABASTRON OF FORGOTTEN GODS

Can Cairo Jim recover the Alabastron of Forgotten Gods in time to save the world? What *is* an alabastron, anyway? Is Euripides Doodah getting tired of people saying "My, oh my, what a wonderful day"? All will be revealed in Cairo Jim's fourth fulminating exploit!

The Cairo Jim Chronicles, read by Geoffrey McSkimming, are available on CD from Bolinda Audio Books! See **www.bolinda.com** for details.